# THE
# LAST
# HURRAH

# THE LAST HURRAH

JEFFERY L. COFFEY

XULON PRESS

Xulon Press
2301 Lucien Way #415
Maitland, FL 32751
407.339.4217
www.xulonpress.com

Paperback ISBN-13: 978-1-6628-5008-0
Hard Cover ISBN-13: 978-1-6628-5009-7

This book is dedicated to the Father, Son, and Holy Spirt that guides our family's lives daily. It is also dedicated to my wife Anna Marie, my children and my grandchildren.

# Introduction

When I am not hiking and foraging with my wife Anna Marie or spending time with our five grown children and ten grandchildren, I am reading about, playing, or watching sports. I started watching sports with my dad when I was five years old. We watched or listened to every North Carolina Tar Heels game, every Washington Redskins game, later it became every Carolina Panthers game, every Nascar race, and the list went on. I played sports in Junior High, High School, College, and semi-professionally. I have coached football, baseball, and basketball at numerous levels. I have played fantasy sports since 1983. I have attended many live sporting events in my lifetime. The reason for me presenting these facts is so you, the reader, can see that I have loved sports all of my life and sports has played a large part in the person I am today.

When I first had the idea of writing a fictional account about the demise of sports in America, it was because I was losing interest in most sports due to all of the negative aspects of professional and college sports. At one time in my life, not that many years ago, I watched the National Football League (NFL), National Basketball Association (NBA), Major League Baseball (MLB), tennis, golf, soccer boxing, Nascar racing, and most college sports. My wife said I would have watched two flies race up a wall if that was all that was on. Today....well that's a different story, I watch zero Nascar, haven't watched an NBA game in eight years, I don't watch any golf, tennis, boxing, or soccer. I haven't watched a MLB game in 12 years. So basically, I watch NFL and college football and basketball. After talking to other sports fans and friends, I realized that there were many others just like me. There are some that actually gave up watching any sports or attending any sporting events. The reasons they gave were many. The reasons ranged from anger over player strikes, player protests, cost of attending games, outrage over scandals, players political involvement, and just plain loss of interest.

If you don't believe there is a loss of interest in sports in America, all you have to do is talk to people ranging in age from twelve to thirty and see how many watch, play, or care about sports. In the 1990's small communities had forty youth football players on a team with four teams within a twenty mile radius, a total of one hundred and sixty players. Today those four communities have to combine to put together one thirty player team.

The more I delved into sports in America and it's history, the more I realized how fragile its existence really is. This story is told through the eyes of Joe Mills a long time sports writer and Pulitzer Prize winner, Floyd Beal a cantankerous ninety year old sportscaster, and Shaun O'Leary a billionaire attorney determined to bring sports back to America. I hope you enjoy reading my take on what I believe will cause the eventual demise and possible resurrection of sports in America.

# Chapter I

New York Times sports editor Joseph J. Mills looked at his antique perpetual calendar and realized it was Wednesday December 31, 2029. Exactly one year from his retirement. He remembered his father giving him the hand changed calendar as a gift many years earlier. At first, he thought that it was really difficult when he had to change the days, weeks, and months by hand every month. Later in life he learned to appreciate the novelty calendar as it not only helped him remember the date, it was also an interesting conversation piece. This being his last year as sports editor of the New York Times newspaper, he stole this moment from editing a sports story to daydream about his long career as a sports writer and sports editor. He glanced at his antique oak bookcase given to him by his parents as a high school graduation gift. At the time Joe was disappointed. His friends were receiving cars and cash. All he got was a oak bookcase. He now appreciated the gift. His friends' cars and the cash were long gone by now, but his bookcase still looked like new, well almost like new. He used the bookcase in college and it was the first thing he moved into his office after being hired to write for the Times so naturally it had suffered some wear. Front and center of the bookcase stood his Pulitzer Prize winning book "The Demise, the Collapse of Sports in America". He won his Pulitzer Prize in the commentary category. It was still hard for him to believe that so many people were interested in the demise of professional sports and college sports in America. Over a million copies of his book had been sold to date. He'd had interviews on over a hundred television and internet media outlets, and had more than a million followers on Twitter PLUS. The prior year Joe had conducted the second most guest speaking appearances and lectures in America. Joe's book was full of facts about each professional league and what eventually led to each one's demise. Joe's daydream came to an abrupt halt when Paul Wiseman lead editor of the newspaper knocked on his door with a request. "Joe, I really want to see something special from the sports team to celebrate the new decade and your last year here. You know that our sports fans are reeling from the loss of the traditional sports they came to know and expected to see every year. Every fan knew that in January there would be college bowl games, in February there would be a Super Bowl and Super Bowl parties. In March there was college basketball's March Madness and brackets to fill out. You know Joe, nobody ever picked a perfect bracket and now there probably won't be any more games to pick from". Joe wasn't so sure about that. There was an attorney in the same building as the Times that had spent several years working for parents, student athletes and college boards trying to persuade the Supreme Court to lift the ban on college athletics. Wiseman continued "Once March Madness was over there was baseball and the NBA playoffs". Joe jokingly responded to his editor by reminding him that there were still other sports to enjoy. "Wiseman, you know there are still sports being played all over America, right? If you'd like you can cover tonight's soccer, oh I meant futbol game for me tonight" His boss wasn't amused. "I realize we still have soccer, hockey, golf and tennis but really how many people cared about those sports until the others were gone? I know there were some fans of those sports but percentage wise it was very low compared to the NFL, NBA, MLB, college football and college basketball. My first thought was to print a different chapter from your book each month but I realized that most sports fans had already read your book and anyway I'm really looking for something on a more positive note. I'm leaving it up to you Joe. I just want something that will take our readers back to a better day when sports in America thrived. " Joe agreed to take on the project but he had no idea how he'd proceed. It'd be hard to put a positive spin on what had happened to sports from 2020-2028. Later that evening while having dinner with his wife Bea, short for Beatrice, he told her about his conversation with Mr. Wiseman. Without pausing she responded, "You should call Floyd and see if he'll do a history of sports from his perspective. After all he's witnessed more than any of your readers. He could talk about happier times." Joe took another bite of chicken pie, then another. He said "That's an excellent idea. The only problem will be convincing him to do it. You know Floyd will be ninety in January and he's not happy with sports in our country or our country itself right now. But I'll give him a call tomorrow. By the way its ideas like that one that makes me keep you around" he joked with his wife of over forty years. "That and this chicken pie".

Joe normally took Sundays off when his job would allow but he had work to do. He entered his office, made a cup of coffee and thought about how he'd convince Floyd Beal to take on such a large project for him and the sports fans of New York. He knew Floyd didn't need the income so there was no sense offering him money. Floyd Beal although famous was a simple man with simple needs. A country boy at heart. Maybe he'd do it just to bring a little joy to the fans that'd heard him announce sports the past forty years. Joe picked up the phone to call Floyd "Rocket" Beal.

On the penthouse floor in an office twenty -eight floors above Joe's office was the office of Attorney Shaun O'Leary. An office that could only be described as eccentric and futuristic. It was occupied by one of the richest men in the United States. O'Leary had just received Joseph J. Mills Pulitzer Prize winning book from a friend that recommended he read it as a means to assist him in his quest to create a new and successful professional baseball league. He opened The Demise to Chapter 1: " O'Leary read:

# Chapter II

"The average Joe in America misses the sports that Americans took for granted for years. Trust me, I'm average and my name is Joe so I know what the average Joe thinks. I believe that most of us really miss the sports we grew up with. No more tailgating, no more fantasy sports, no more team jerseys, no more drafts, no more March Madness, no more world champions, no more fans, no more coaches, no more super stars, no more National Football League, no more National Basketball Association, no more Major League Baseball, no more college football bowls or basketballs March Madness, all vanished. Unless you love soccer, hockey, tennis or golf your no longer an American sports fan. I believe people thought that sports in America would last forever. What they failed to realize was that in reality sports in America was not as old as fans believed. They also failed to realize how fragile the popularity of sports could be when people become greedy, politically motivated, or even when a pandemic strikes the country. While greed probably started sports downfall, a pandemic in 2020, politics, wide spread corruption, negative fan reaction to protests all contributed to the collapse of professional sports as we once knew it. If you look at the life span of each sport that's no longer a part of our American culture, it's still hard for the average Joe to believe that sports could and did collapse. Some of the most anticipated and watched events were now a thing of the past. Therefore, former fans were forced to find other things to do and spend their entertainment dollars on, unless however you are a fan of the before mentioned sports. Who dreamed that by 2027 soccer or futbol as its now referred would be the most popular sport in America and the world?

Most fans tended to believe that professional and college sports in America were here from the beginning of time and had a long-life span? This is just not the case. Life spans listed chronologically from the earliest, the demise of Nascar to the last sport to fall, Major League Baseball gives a glimpse into the fragility of them all. Nascar racing began on February 1, 1949. It folded on July 4, 2024. It was ironic that the founding of Nascar and the first race were both held in Daytona Beach Florida. In the end the inability to sell even twenty thousand tickets to a race that once sold over two hundred thousand tickets, spelled the end of Nascar in 2025. So Nascar lasted a total of seventy six years. Not even the average life span of a person in America. That's eighty years. The next to fold was the National Football League or NFL. The NFL was founded in 1899 as the American Professional Football Association. It became the NFL in 1922. The NFL folded in 2025 so it lasted one hundred and three years. Following the NFL, the next to face the demise was collegiate sports and the National Collegiate Athletic Association or NCAA. The NCAA was founded in 1910 and was active until 2026 when the Supreme Court suspended any intercollegiate sports until a decision could be made on Rule IX after college football and basketball could no longer support all of the other athletic teams. The NCAA survived one hundred and eighteen years. My grandmother if still alive would be much older than the NCAA. There is still hope among fans and alumni that college sports will return in the future, but it's been three years with no real progress. The NBA was founded in New York in 1946. The league folded in New York in 2027 after an eighty one-year -old history. When the NBA failed, fans could not believe that the league was only eighty one years old. They acted like the league had been around for two hundred years. The first to come was the last to go. Major League Baseball was founded in 1871 and folded in 2027, a run of one hundred and fifty six years, by far the oldest of all the sports. It's no wonder baseball lasted longest as it was always known as America's game. I will examine the demise of each league and Association in detail throughout this book but I thought it was important for you to have a timeline. Sports in America have not been around forever. Nascar, NFL, MLB, NBA, and NCAA combined had an average life span of one hundred and thirteen years. That's not very old for something that many Americans enjoyed and expected to be around forever more. Sadly, this wasn't the case.

# Chapter III

As Shaun O'Leary continued to read the introduction of the book, he realized he didn't really know much about Joe Mills other than he was a award winning sportswriter and now successful author. Despite his lack of knowledge about Joe, Joe's story was one of great accomplishments. Joe Mills was in his forty eighth and final year covering and editing sports stories for the New York Times. Today Joe had volunteered to cover a National Futbol League game between the New York Liberty and Chicago Breeze. Joe was covering this assignment only because a colleague's son was celebrating a birthday and Joe didn't really have anything else to do. Not in his opinion anyway, wife Bea had plenty for him to do. Joe really didn't have to cover anything he didn't want to at this point in his career. After all, he won five national literary awards and received that Pulitzer Prize for his book. The book delved into what caused the demise of each particular sport and league. It was published in 2028 the year after our final major professional sport, major league baseball folded and closed its doors. Being seventy years old Joe started with the newspaper in 1975 as a fifteen-year-old delivering papers door to door. As a kid Mills known then only as Joe hoped for a career in sports. He attended St. John's University where he earned a degree in sports journalism and another in religious studies. Joe Mills was never an athlete but that didn't prevent him from being the most educated sports fan in his school. His love of sports didn't come from his family. Joe's father was a minister and didn't have much time for anything else. His father did however enjoy keeping up with sports and read the New York newspaper sports section every morning. In his father's opinion his and everybody else time should be spent on education, reading, and the arts and not so much on sports. While he said he just kept up with sports for conversation purposes Joe thought his father actually enjoyed it. Of course, there was the daily bible study. Joe didn't mind the strict religious upbringing, he felt like the lessons he learned in life from his parents and the education they afforded him was invaluable. Joe also knew that he was not an athlete by any stretch of the imagination. After all its hard to be an athlete when at eighteen years of age your five feet and six inches tall and weigh a whopping one hundred and sixty five pounds. Despite the odds of Joe Mills loving sports being slim, his love grew day by day. Joe may not have been able to compete on the field or on the court but nobody could compete with Joe when it came to his knowledge of statistics, records, and analysis of the world of sports. Joe Mills loved every sport. Growing up Joe could not watch the games on television as his father did not allow a television in his home but he followed it through the newspaper and week-old Sporting News magazines that church member Cecil Thomas saved for him each week. His father insisted that Joe attend St. John's University to earn his degree in religious education and follow in his footsteps to become a priest or religious educator. Joe didn't balk at the idea knowing that his major might be in religious education because he knew his minor would be in sports journalism. Joe could have never imagined the joy he'd find in watching live sporting events. He'd never seen a game in person. He'd only been able to watch games at a friend's house. Joe would become St. John's University campus sports editor as a sophomore. This distinction was normally reserved for seniors but Joe's impressive and tireless efforts as a freshman led to him earning this early distinction as a sophomore. During his freshman year he'd volunteer to cover any and all events. If there was a croquet tournament Joe covered it. If there was a badminton tournament Joe would cover it. Joe would cover any event he had a chance to write about. Joe would graduate from St. John's University with honors with two degrees, religious education and sports journalism. Joe had known for years that eventually he'd have to tell his father Rev. Ralph Mills that he wouldn't be entering the religious field and instead would enter the world of covering and writing about sports. Joe hoped that the fact that the New York Times newspaper had already offered him a paid internship would soften the blow when he had to tell Rev. Mills of his plans. Joe told the story many times of how he told his dad of his plans. Over the years the story became a part of his speeches and was afforded space in his Pulitzer Prize winning book's introduction. The story went like this: Joe's father and mother had planned a surprise graduation party at their house. Guest would include friends, family, and members of St. Peter Church. Rev. Mills had a surprise for Joe Mills. He'd already received permission from the church and its board for Joe Mills to replace the recently retired youth educational minister at the church's school. Little did Rev. Mills know the surprise would be on him. Joe and his mother had a different relationship from he and his father. She was supportive of anything he undertook and would be just as happy with him being a sportswriter as a priest or religious educator. As long as Joe was happy, his mom was happy for him. Joe spent the afternoon with his mom shopping, not knowing she was keeping him away so the surprise party could be prepared and the guest could arrive. Joe was totally surprised by the party and totally unprepared for the announcement that Rev. Mills would make moments later that afternoon. As soon as the surprise part of the party concluded Rev Mills was ready to make his announcement. He stood in front of the large stone fireplace where many fires were started for warmth over the years. He said "I have a special announcement to make. This will not only be a surprise for all of you but a surprise and the graduation gift of a lifetime for our son Joe. I made a recommendation to the church board that we hire my son Joe to replace the retiring Dr. Emerson as Director of Youth Education at St. Peter's School effective in sixty days". Joe's mouth dropped open as the entire party applauded and started congratulating Joe. Joe was speechless. What was he going to do now? In sixty days, he'd be starting his new religious education job, or so his dad thought. He decided it was best not to say anything during the party about the newspaper job. After all he had two months before his religious education job would begin. That'd buy him a little time to tell his dad without ruining his day and the party he'd planned for his son. The following month Joe started his internship at the newspaper. He was assigned to work with writer Paul Worth covering the World Series between the St. Louis Cardinals and the Milwaukee Brewers. It wasn't unusual for Joe to visit friends and attend games together so it wouldn't be suspicious to his parents that he was out of town at a baseball game. The first two games were in St. Louis and Joe was amazed at the pageantry and planning that a sporting event of this magnitude would demand. Joe also couldn't believe that the reporters had such great suites and amazing food at the stadium. Covering college sports, he ate whatever he could fit in his brief case. Most of the time that equated to peanut butter sandwiches or left overs from the night before. He walked slowly by the buffet and saw everything from hamburgers and chicken wings to sushi and banana splits. He tried a little of each and a lot of some! During the games Joe took notes about every pitch and hit during the first four games. Mr. Worth was so impressed by Joe that he allowed him to write the game five World Series article and assign his name to it. On Thursday evening Joe covered the game and was excited that it was a pivotal game as the series was tied at two games apiece. It was an exciting game not only because he was excited to be there but the game came down to the last inning with the Brewers holding on to win 6-4 to take a three games to two lead in the series. After the game Joe set in the suite and wrote his first article for the Times while downing his forth or maybe fifth French pastry of the evening. His first article would appear in the October 18th, morning edition. Joe knew his dad read the New York Times newspaper from front to back every day, but figured he didn't look at who had written each article. After all the writers name was in very small print. His dad only read the sports so he could keep up with current events the church members talked about., he said. The excitement of his first assignment prevented him from worrying about his dad's reaction if he read the article. It wasn't until later in the evening that he realized "well my dad's going to see that article in the morning"! He thought he could always do what Lucy did on the I love Lucy show he'd watched recently. He could just cut the article out of the newspaper but it'd probably turn out just like it did for Lucy, not good. Joe decided that he'd remove the entire sports section the following morning before Rev. Mills had a chance to read it. It'd be a hard task as his dad had a routine that included getting up at five thirty and the first thing he did was get his paper and make coffee. Joe's flight wouldn't get back to New York until one thirty in the morning. He wouldn't get home until two thirty or three o'clock and he'd have to get up at five and retrieve the newspaper from the driveway before Rev. Mills had time to get it. The alarm clock rang at four forty five and Joe was up! He raced out of his room passing by his parents' room to get to the door. Joe thought that worst case scenario would be he'd remove the sports section in the driveway. While he was excited to see his name in print in the New York Times for the first time he was just as apprehensive about his dad seeing his name on the article. He went outside and of course the paper was late. The driveway was empty. He went back into the kitchen and watched out the window for the headlights belonging to the delivery person. He thought back eight years earlier and how he had prided himself on having the papers at the customers residences on time. Rev. Mills told him early on that these people have jobs. They want to have their coffee and newspaper before they leave for work. It was part of their routine. Well our newspaper deliverer didn't seem to have the same work ethic or maybe he had car trouble. Who knows but all Joe knew was that he needed that paper to get there. As he finished his thoughts, he saw headlights approaching and heard his dad's alarm clock go off. In a minute or two his dad would be entering the room wondering why Joe was already up. After what seemed like eternity the car pulled up in front of his house and he heard the paper hit the ground. Joe thought "God really does answer prayers". He ran out and picked up the paper. As he entered the house he saw the lights on in his parents' room. He took the paper in the house and went back into his room. As he quietly closed the door he heard his father's voice "Joe, are you up?" Joe froze and said "yea I've got some things I have to do early this morning". He was finally in his room with the newspaper. Before he took the sports section out he had to read his first published article. Before he could read the first word he heard his dad complaining about the paper being late. Joe took the sports section out of the paper and hid it under his pillow. He took the paper in the kitchen. Joe smelled the coffee his dad was making. He never liked coffee or had even tried it until he was covering sports at St. John's University. After covering a big badminton match and getting home at two am. coffee came in handy then. He actually learned to like it with lots of cream and sugar. He walked into the kitchen and handed his dad the newspaper minus the sports section. Within a few minutes Rev Mills said that the sports section was missing. Joe told him he had taken it out to read earlier. "Now what "? Joe thought. That's when Joe decided it was time to tell his dad the truth. He returned from his room and handed his dad the missing article. Well so much for him not looking at the writer. Almost immediately he asked "you wrote this for the newspaper"? All Joe could do was nod his head yes. His dad immediately knew that his son was not going into religious education and his smile and tears of joy shocked Joe. Rev. Mills hugged Joe and told him "I'm proud of you son, I want you to go on to become the best sportswriter ever". He yelled for his wife, and the Rev. rarely yelled, but he wanted her to come and read the article. Mrs. Mills came running out to see what all the commotion was about. She wasn't typically an early riser. When she heard the news, she put her hands on her hips and told Rev. Mills, "I tried to tell you, this boy was meant to cover sports"! This was not the response he expected but Joe was happier than he'd ever been, the mascaraed was over. Rev. Mills had no problem filling the religious education position and Joe was happy about that. Now there would be no guilt for him following his love of sports. Later on, Rev and Mrs. Mills would witness him win and accept the Pulitzer Prize among his many other awards. Joe knew deep down he'd never have accomplished as much or effected as many lives as a religious educator as he had as a sportswriter. Rev. Mills never mentioned the religious education position to Joe again after he read that first article. Rev. Mills read his son's articles every morning at five thirty sharp. He showed Joe's articles to everyone who'd read them for the next twenty-four years before he passed away. Joe always thought this was a great story to tell because he felt it showed how dreams can come true and obstacles overcome.

Joe's first year 1982 was a year of on the job training tagging along with all of the top sports beat writers for the newspaper. He was fortunate enough that in his first assignment he was invited to join the experienced writers and witnessed every game of a seven game World Series as the St. Louis Cardinals defeated the Milwaukee Brewers four games to three. Joe helped cover the 1983 NFL Super Bowl watching the Washington Redskins defeat the Miami Dolphins for their first ever Super Bowl title. Joe didn't realize at the time that he would witness many more exciting and historical sporting moments during his career A career soon coming to an end. He would have never dreamed what fate had in store for him.

Before going to cover the soccer game, Joe phoned Floyd Beal. Beal didn't own a cell phone, just an old rotary dial phone from the 1960's. So, if Floyd wasn't at his house, you weren't going to talk to him. There was a reason that Joe's wife had suggested that his friend Rocket Beal whom they called Floyd write the historical articles. He and Floyd were best of friends and had witnessed so many of the same events over the years.

Joe Mills met Rocket Beal for the first time in 1998 and immediately they hit it off. Joe was writing about games while Rocket was announcing them. After the games they'd go out and have a beer or ten while talking about everything including sports. Floyd Beal was proud of Joe and his book and all the awards he won although he was still soured on the issues that led to many of his beloved sports being dissolved. While Joe felt like his book was full of facts and opinions he never thought the book presented the rich history that each league deserved. While Rocket Beal was also very attached to sports in a professional manner he was also the biggest fan that Joe had ever met. He had encouraged Beal to write a book of his own but the old man wasn't interest. Today though he'd decided to approach Beal about doing a series of articles on what he'd seen in his lifetime and in the world of sports. That'd include the history that made each sport successful until the demise. Joe knew without a doubt that the articles would be entertaining for all and would certainly light up the editorial pages. Floyd "Rocket" Beal had no problem giving his opinion whether you wanted it or not. He was never one to back down. You can ask any batter that a one hundred mile per hour fastball whizzed by their heads how tough he was. After three or four rings Manna answered the phone. Manna was a live-in caregiver that had lived with Beal for six years. She cooked, cleaned, shopped for and kept Beal company after the passing of Beal's wife. Floyd Beal's wife passed away ten years earlier after a long battle with Alzheimer's. Joe was happy to hear Manna's voice. She was an angel of a lady and tolerated Floyd's old-time way of life. He thought she actually enjoyed it. "Hey Ms. Manna, its Joe, how have you been". She answered "I know who this is! Its great hearing from you, how's Bea doing?" "She's great! She has me doesn't she" both laughing out loud. "How's Floyd doing?" he asked. " He's taking a nap right now but he's not doing good Joe. In May he was diagnosed with the early onset of Alzheimer's . I shouldn't tell you this but he's also started back on the Moonshine. Real heavy on the Moonshine. He's been really depressed since the diagnosis. You know what he went through with Helen." Joe was stunned! Why hadn't his friend called him? But that's just how Beal was. The conversation ended and Manna promised to have Floyd call him later that day. Four hours later the phone rang. It was Floyd Beal. The two spoke for a while. Joe approached Floyd with his idea of having him write a series of articles based on events he'd witnessed in his life time. Beal was not interested at all. "Hell no Joe, I ain't interested in working anymore" Several days later he had lunch at Joe's house and Bea heated up the leftover chicken pie. While Joe went to the kitchen to make drinks Bea explained to Floyd Beal how much it'd mean to Joe if he'd write the articles. Beal promised her he'd think about it. After further coaxing from Ms. Manna he phoned Joe and said he'd be happy to do this for him, sports fans across America but mainly to keep the peace with Bea and Manna. "I'll tell them about the good old days" he quipped. It was agreed that the articles would begin within the following month and culminate with Floyd's birthday in November 2029.

# Chapter IV

S haun O'Leary looked online at the New York Times newspaper website. He looked forward to reading Rocket Beal's initial article and looked forward to reading more just so he could get another brilliant opinion of what happened to sports in America. The articles along with Joe Mills book continued to educate him on how and why sports in America lost its fan bases and failed to survive. He had his own reasons for the interest he took in the subject. O'Leary, known to his friends and colleagues as Shaun, was just thirty-eight years old in 2024 when auto racing folded all of its operations. He was very disappointed that any sport enjoyed by so many people and employing so many people would just fold its operations. O'Leary was born into a wealthy sport loving family. He and his family attended many live sporting events having season tickets to the Giants NFL team, the Knicks NBA team, and the Yankees major league baseball team. Over the next ten years Shaun would witness the demise of Nascar the NFL, MLB, NBA and all college sports despite his strong support and love for each and every one of those sports. Shaun O'Leary attended Harvard University and like his father before him and his grandfather and his great grandfather, he became a high-profile attorney and sports agent with offices in New York City, Miami, Chicago and Los Angeles He represented many famous athletes and entertainers in contract negotiations and other matters as needed. Over the next 5 years following the collapse of auto racing he would slowly witness the demise of the NFL, NBA, college sports, and finally his favorite, Major League Baseball. The demise and eventual collapse of the most popular professional sports and all college sports in America had put a huge dent in the attorney's income. It didn't really matter, with inheritances, high profile client's, and good investments Mr. O'Leary was a billionaire many times over before age 35, and his wealth only increased over the years thanks to a thing called Bitcoin. Now in 2029 he was one of the wealthiest men in the United States. With time on his hands, O'Leary now forty five years old spent his days and nights circulating plans to bring sports back to America. Not all sports but the ones he felt could survive during these crazy times in America. He felt that each sport failed due to its own short comings and internal greed by owners and players could have been avoided. When he saw that the New York newspaper was running a series of articles about the history of sports in America, he felt this was the opportune time to convince the public that college and professional sports were positive things for individuals, families, and the nation itself. He'd wanted to use this opportunity, his wealth and political clout to reach his goal of bringing professional and college sports back to America! He wasn't sure exactly where he'd start. He felt like baseball might be the easiest to promote and he had many ideas as to how things should be run. He'd first have to find a way to attract owners. This didn't seem to be a major obstacle. People missed baseball, it was simple as that. The biggest obstacle would be convincing players that were now playing in Japan and other countries to return home to play in a brand-new league for less money. He figured that with no college baseball, and no minor leagues, the talent may not be the best but it would be entertaining. On the back burner he'd work on the return of NCAA sports. He had a plan for that also. The NBA return would depend on how successful his plan for baseball was. There would be no return of the NFL, just too many obstacles to overcome. As for Nascar, Shaun never thought there would be enough sponsors or drivers to start up the sport again operating as it once had. The small southern racing circuit continued to draw huge numbers. Fans were able to watch hometown racing and hometown heroes every week, not something they had to save a year for to see one race. Shaun O'Leary started making a to do list to begin his quest of bringing back Major League Baseball to America. "Contact potential board members, contact potential baseball owners in twelve major cities. Hire a company to develop a name, a brand, and a logo and promote the new league. Contact stadiums and cities about the possibility of bringing a team to the city. The list became longer and longer but now the goal seemed obtainable. At least this list written on a napkin at Big Un's was a start. After he returned to his office he opened his laptop and read Rocket Beal's introduction to the upcoming articles.

# Chapter V

August 15, 2029 "Rocket" Beal wrote for the New York Times: " By the time I complete these articles my family will be celebrating my ninetieth birthday, if I live that long. I was born in 1940. Wow am I really this old, this quick? Ten years from now I guess I'll officially be an old man. I have been asked by this fine newspaper's sports editor Joe Mills, a dear friend, colleague, and beer buddy of mine for many years to provide a series of articles of historic events I've witnessed. He thinks his online or in my opinion outta line readers would be interested in what I have witnessed and learned over my nearly ninety year journey. A journey that saw my life transform from a poor farmers son in Tennessee to an All-American baseball player with a professional baseball career spanning over ten years. That was followed by a forty-year broadcasting career, followed by twenty-two years of retirement. Initially, I hesitated about providing this series of articles because my handwriting diminished long ago, not that anyone can read cursive writing or even printing for that matter anymore. But Joe's wife and her chicken pie convinced me to take on this project. I know nothing about those new-fangled computers. It took me long enough to learn how to use old fangled computers. Now the damn things talk to you. I know nothing about internet or interspace or whatever it's called now. I know nothing about I Phone 102 or 104, or whatever number they are on now. Never understood why it was an I phone. Why not an A phone? Isn't A the best grade? Well maybe that's changed too. Anyway, my friend Joe insisted I do the series of articles and he said he'd provide me with one of those fancy contraptions, can't remember what he called it. A mini mike or something. All I have to do is talk and the robot as small as a thimble, (do you folks even know what a thimble is?) will transcribe what I am saying directly to the newspaper office. I thought if all I have to do is talk...I can do that. I'm really good at talking. You don't announce sports for forty years if you don't like talking, right? I still don't understand why he thinks anybody cares anything about what I think. He said it's because I've seen a lot of things and I have many interesting opinions on the events I've been witness to. I thought this over for a while and decided to do this because I really have witnessed some great things and some not so great in my time, not only in sports but in the entire nation. I imagine the best way for me to translate my thoughts and keep them accurate is to use ten and twenty year increments as a basis for facts. The first in the series of eight will be my life from 1940-1960, the first twenty years of my life. I realize that I may not have many years left to share my life's events with others, so now is as good of time as any. After all, ninety years old is a long life. My goal is to not only give you a historical account of sports but also to inform you and others about non-sports topics so you'll know the truth of what has happened over my lifetime, not some fantasy the "system" says you need to learn. I know Joe Mills only ask me for a sports article but I figure now, what the heck, lets really let loose. Let me try to introduce myself to you so you'll have a better understanding when you read the upcoming articles. In my articles you won't be told nonsense like that Native Americans welcomed the Pilgrims with open arms and they all happily celebrated the first Thanksgiving with festive moods sharing food, drink, and laughter Actually and factually they fought each other from the start and the "Pilgrims" eventually stole the Native Americans land. I'm sure there was no thanksgiving celebration. Same with many historical events including the world of sports. There was cheating and conniving in the world of sports in every decade. All the way back to the White Sox scandal in 1909, one hundred and twenty years ago. I don't want the youth or even the adults of today to be so mis educated the way my generation and many of those following mine were misguided, misinformed and lied to. Oh, by the way, in case you haven't noticed,

I'm not....what do they call it? Politically correct. My articles will probably be more edited than any in the history of this New York Times newspaper. I was born in the deep woods of Tennessee on Thanksgiving Day, November 1940. In my years, I have seen history transformed from the days when there was no FM radio and only two AM stations (let me guess you don't know what AM is either... geez) We didn't have nine hundred television channels, do they still call it television? I don't know nothing anymore in this crazy world. How the hell did a woman become a man, a man become a woman, some are both and they all use the same restroom? There's a hundred different genders? I thought God just made two. Oh well that's for a different decade. I'll get to that soon enough. The fact is we had three television stations CBS,NBC, and ABC. We also had something called UHF that provided a local channel, when it was working, which was not very often. The networks signed off at twelve midnight and came back on at six in the morning. If you stayed up after midnight you watched a test screen all night. What's a test screen? Get off your reality game and look it up, it'll do you good. I remember the assassination of President John F. Kennedy, the first "moon walk", the assassination of Martin Luther King and many other important historical events. I remember listening to radio drama and comedy shows and radio game shows. After the shows were over and Guy Lombardo played his last tune of the night the radio tuner was tuned in to sporting events. In the 1950's and 1960's, listening to boxing bouts between great heavy weights of the time was one of the old folks' favorite things to do on a late Saturday night . Joe Lewis, Rocky Marciano, Floyd Patterson all great people and great fighters. The baseball World Series was the biggest sports radio event of the year and was played during the day, as were all games at the time. Despite living through and experiencing much so history in my life, the most important and unexpected events of all to me was the slow forty year deterioration and eventual elimination of most professional and college sports in America. I was a sports fan all of my life not only as a player and announcer but enjoying live sporting events with my children and grandchildren and watching them on television. ? The decline of sports began in America in 2024 when Nascar, Indy, and NHRA drag racing all disbanded. While it didn't surprise me that car racing started the decline of sports in America, I never imagined that within five more years there would be no more NFL, NBA, and no more college sports. Hockey, tennis, golf and soccer all survived. As I approach my articles I will be touching on the decline of sports in our country I might even throw in a couple of politically incorrect opinions along the way. Look forward to my first article August 15...same bat time, same bat channel... (just forget it, just something from my past.)

Floyd "Rocket" Beal was born on Thanksgiving Day 1940 to Floyd and Belle Beal in the farm country of Tennessee. His parents had nine other children and survived by selling apples and sweet corn to local stores on Saturdays. They made the long trip to Knoxville to sell the fruits (and vegetables) of their labor. During his childhood Beal would get up at five in the morning and farm until seven when he left for a mile-long walk to school. One thing Floyd Beal demanded was that all of his children get a formal education. He'd say "Farming is a hard life, I want your lives to be easier than mine". As a result Rocket not only went to college but he went for free. He was the first person to throw a baseball over a hundred miles per hour leading to the name "Rocket". In 1958 he would be named a college All-American while leading the Tennessee Volunteers to its one and only college World Series. The following year he would sign a contract to play for the Boston Red Sox. Rocket played for ten years in the major leagues. He retired in 1969 due to an injury that years later would be called a "Tommy John" injury. Rocket used his notoriety as a seven-time all-star and his journalism degree from Tennessee and parlayed them into a very successful sportscasting career. Despite a busy schedule including Olympic Games, NFL, MLB, NBA and NCAA games, Rocket found time to marry and raise three children of his own. Two boys and a girl brought Rocket a total of eleven grandchildren, which produced 6 great grandchildren. He was very proud of each child, grandchild, and great grandchild. Rocket always said his biggest regret was that despite his great grandchildren being exceptional athletes they were never able to take advantage of their talents as NCAA college sports shut its doors several years before any of Rockets great grandchildren were able to take advantage of their athletic abilities and talents. While Rocket seemed to be a gruff opinionated old man, which he was, he was dearly loved by all of his family and friends. He was now preparing to write the first article in the series.

# Chapter VI

Sports fans and former sports fans, its time to delve into the history of sports,(and other topics) as I remember them. I'll start with the first twenty years of my life.

I don't remember much from 1940 to 1955 probably because I was busy growing both mentally and physically and working my ass off on the family farm. During those formative year's sports played very little part of my life as my time was spent helping on the family farm. From 1955 to 1960 I remember a lot about sports and about what was happening all over our great nation. When I was 15 years old I remember my parents talking about how some lady in Alabama refused to sit in the back of bus and it was a big deal. I remember thinking "what's the big deal?" Front of the bus, back of the bus, who cares? Much later in life I'd learn this was Rosa Parks and the importance of her stance and the courage it had taken her to sit in the front of that bus. The following year 1956 I heard my family and their friends complaining about a singer from Memphis Tennessee that they didn't want any of the kids watching or listening to because he sang Rock and Roll music and shook his hips a lot. That man would become the greatest music success of all time. You may have heard of him; his name was Elvis Presley. At this point please don't try to compare any of today's musicians electronic or solar sonic or whatever it's called, to Elvis or the Beatles for that matter. It'd be an insult to both. Their music is 80 years old and still listened to today. My great grandsons still sing one of Elvis's first hits "you ain't nothing but a hound dog". As far as sports was concerned, and that's the topic I'll be mainly concentrating on in this series since I was a sports announcer. I can't tell you much about politics, music, television, or historic events but I can tell you all about sports because I was there. During my life time I saw the greatest of the greatest in every sport. From 1950 through 1955 I don't really remember anything but since it was in my lifetime I feel compelled to tell you what was going on. In 1950 the NFL (National Football League) combined with the AAFC and added three teams. One of those teams was the Cleveland Browns. The AAFC would later become the American Football League which eventually led to the creation of the Super Bowl of professional football. In Major League baseball the Yankees won their thirteenth world championship. In the first NBA dynasty the Minneapolis Lakers won its second straight title with George Mikan leading the way. George was a story of his own. Mikan was the first big man of basketball and actually changed the rules of the game forever. As a kid Mikan spent a year and a half in bed with a shattered knee. Mikan never seemed destined to become an athlete. When Mikan entered Chicago's DePaul University in 1942, he stood six feet ten inches and weighed two hundred forty pounds, moved awkwardly because of his frame and his childhood surgeries. He also wore thick glasses for his near-sightedness. Mikan was approached by head basketball coach Ray Meyer who convinced Mikan to come out for the college team. He then taught Mikan how to shoot the hook shot. Mikan would go on to become a three-time college All-American and a dominating professional player. Mikans shot blocking near the rim led to college and professional basketball adopting the goal tending rule that remained effective until college and professional basketball died.1957 brought forth the next two great big men of the game. Thirteen-time NBA champion Bill Russell played his first season of professional basketball. Wilt Chamberlin the only player to score a hundred points in a professional game finished his college career at Kansas. His final collegiate game was one of the most famous in college hoops history as his undefeated Kansas Jayhawks lost to the also undefeated University of North Carolina 59-57 in triple overtime. In 1954 Nascar was only seven years old but had become so popular that one hundred thirty six cars started in the Daytona 500. Yes, over a hundred cars and the race was run on the beach. Five years later in 1959 Daytona International Speedway opened and the race was no longer run on the beach. In 1958 the National Football League held what would become known as "the greatest game ever played". It was the NFL Championship game won by the Baltimore Colts as they defeated the New York Giants in sudden death overtime. This was a game of first. It was the first championship game to go into sudden death overtime. More importantly it was the first nationally televised professional football game. We all packed up in the farm truck and drove to a friend of our family and watched the game. Despite it being the "greatest game ever", I'd have to disagree with that. As I continue this series I'll let you know of many games greater and more exciting than this one. This was one of the first real sports memories I had. Of course, the team I pulled for, the Giants, lost. Don't ask me why I pulled for the Giants, I guess I just liked their name better. That became a constant over my lifetime, my team usually loses. The Giants lost to the Colts again in the 1959 title game.

As for popularity of each sport, The NFL gained quite a following in the 1950's. From 1950 until 1959 the NFL grew by over a million fans growing from two million in 1950 to over three million in 1959. Television coverage of the NFL in the 1950's were the most pivotal years in history. In 1951 the first live coast to coast broadcast occurred when the NFL Championship was televised by Dumont. In 1952, only New York Giants games were televised by Dumont. Dumont was one of the pioneers in the commercial television network industry. It rivaled NBC and CBS for distinction of being the first network television. By 1959 only large market teams had games televised, the small market teams were completely ignored. So, television revenue was almost nonexistent for the NFL. The increase in attendance and the increased marketing of memorabilia served to provide sufficient income for most teams to continue to exist.

The NBA didn't look like it'd survive the decade. Between 1950 and 1959 three teams folded leaving the NBA with only eight teams. Despite the league only having eight teams, owners still worked to find ways to increase interest and attendance Thanks to some of those ideas including the twenty four second clock, attendance was starting to rise. In the 1950's NBA attendance rose from just below five thousand per game to over sixty five hundred per game in 1959. In 1953 and 1954 the NBA signed its first television contract with Dumont.

Major League Baseball was up and down. Total attendance in 1950 was seventeen million. By 1959 it increased to nineteen million. The years in between averaged less than seventeen million. So, you could say that interest in the game remained consistent or you could say it was treading water with no increase in interest or fan base.

College sports in the 1950s was thriving at an all-time high. College football attendance was much larger than the NFL's and once drew over ninety eight thousand fans to a Rose Bowl game. College basketball was much the same with two season ending national tournaments competing with each other. In the 1950's the NIT (National Invitational Tournament) was just as popular if not more so than the NCAA tournament. These two sports even in the 1950's supported all of the other collegiate teams at the school as they did all the way to the end.

With all of that said all of the major sports and leagues were on the upswing by the end of the 1950's decade. This was probably the last decade that would survive without issues that compounded decade after decade until sports as we knew it in the 50's just vanished. That's it for article one. Have a blessed and peaceful day.

The following day after the article was published as with everything in the world, there were comments left by readers that loved the article and those that hated it. One comment said the "old man" had no idea about sports today and needs to go back to the nursing home and quit trying to be an expert at his age. "What's the old man going to know about the hip hop athletes of the past thirty years? Nothing that's what! How can he tell us what happened to sports"? I thought he was going to be controversial with his opinions, this was like a history class, and I never liked history". Joe thought to himself that when Beal saw the comments, he wouldn't be sad, he wouldn't be mad, and his feelings wouldn't be hurt, he'd just laugh. This is the same Rocket that years ago would throw a hundred mile per hour fastball at your head if you disrespected him. Joe was hoping his friend wouldn't take the time to read the comments because he didn't want one of those readers getting plunked in the head with a baseball. He knew in reality that Rocket would read the comments and the next article wouldn't change much because Floyd Beal never veered too far left or right. He'd been around long enough to know how people were and knew not to take things personal but many of the comments were personal and downright mean. "Why does anybody care about this old man's memories, they are probably all made up...can you say dementia?" While there were negative post, there were many more positive comments, "What an amazing article, not only do we get to learn about sports from decades past, we also learn about things that were happening outside the world of sports". Another wrote, I consider myself a huge sports fan that thought I was educated in the world of sports. In Rockets first article I learned so much that I didn't know. Can't wait for the next article". "Who knew Mikan never played basketball until he got to college?" Do you think these positive comments are the comments that will spark ole Rocket before article number two? Probably not. He'd treat them just like the negative ones, with a grain of salt.

Attorney Shaun O'Leary had really enjoyed reading the introduction and the initial article from Beal. They were very informative and he was surprised at all the history he'd missed out on before he was born. Before retiring for the evening O' Leary cracked open Joe Mills book Demise to the next chapter.

# Chapter VII

O'Leary started reading "Nascar was founded in 1948 so the 1950's were years of development of not only the rules but development of the fan base. By 1950 the association was called the Grand National Association. The cars were initially "modified" meaning that they were strictly stock or there was almost no difference in the race car and the car that the everyday person could buy and drive home from their local car dealership. By 1952 Nascar was trying to expand and held its first foreign race in Canada near Niagara Falls. The early years also brought about competition between the big three car makers, Chrysler, Ford, and Chevrolet competed to win races increasing the chances that fans would want to drive the "winning" car as their own mode of transportation. Could anyone now imagine a Studebaker or a Nash on a race track? Attendance and popularity continued to grow as fans and families drove to the local race tracks to see the same model of car racing around a track in excess of a hundred miles per hour that they had driven their family and friends to the race in. Times were generally great for the sport but there were also some not so great times like in 1957 when a race in Newberry SC drew only nine hundred fans. The smallest turnout in history. Nascar was slowly learning that each track had its own success rates and popularity. In 1950 there were nineteen races at twelve different race tracks. By 1959 there were forty two races at over thirty different tracks with a race all the way in Los Angeles, Ca. Nascar racing was looking like the sport of the future.

Anybody that thought that the sport of Nascar's popularity would wane during the 1960's would have been horribly wrong. Anybody that thought that the competition between auto makers would wane would have also been horribly wrong. By 1960 Nascar had constructed super speedways in Charlotte NC, Atlanta, GA, and Hanford CA. Nascar also found its way on to television for the first time in 1960 when CBS televised three of the preliminary races during Daytona Speed week. The competition between auto makers was so intense and competitive that they hired spies to see what their competitors were working on. There was also a lot of history to be made. In 1960 "The King" Richard Petty won for the first time winning at the Charlotte (NC) Fairgrounds at the age of twenty two. He won eight hundred dollars. Petty would win his first Nascar Championship four years later in 1964. The largest payday in 1960 was a little less than twenty thousand dollars awarded to Junior Johnson for winning the Daytona 500. Rumor had it that Johnson made more than that in a week selling his moonshine. To show how popular the sport became in the 1960's all one has to do is look at the attendance of the Daytona 500 throughout the decade. In 1960 thirty nine thousand fans attended the race. By 1969 over a hundred thousand race fans were in attendance. An increase of over sixty three thousand fans. Little did Nascar owners, drivers, and fans know that this total would eventually exceed two hundred thousand attending regularly in its future hay day.

Nascar was billed and rightfully so as the sport of the seventies. While it was true that new facilities were popping up all over the country and the fan base continued to grow there were rumblings behind the scenes. The drivers formed a union in order to get better pay and better conditions. More and more sponsors were interested in Nascar bringing millions more to each race team. The drivers felt like they should have a larger share since they were the ones risking their lives every race day. The top drivers became household names and celebrities. Richard Petty (known as the king of racing) David Pearson, the Yarbrough brothers, the Allison brothers, and many others would help Nascar racing become one of if not the most loved sports in the South East. After all that's where the sport began. In 1979 the first televised Nascar race was run at Daytona. The race ended in fisticuffs between Cale

Yarbrough and the Allison brothers. Talk about a ratings boost. Prior to that race fans would be glued to their radios to listen to the action. Those without radios in their house would sit in their car for 3 hours just to tune in. Nascar continued to flourish. From 1980 through the early 2000's Nascar gained popularity and fans like no other sport in history. In 1998 Nascar attendance was over six million for an average of almost a hundred thousand fans per race. By 2004 the number of fans in attendance had swelled to over eleven million.

It didn't take long for the success of expansion to give way to failure. By 2010 Nascar was starting to lose popularity. The sport began rapid decline in 2010 but by 2013 the falling attendance became apparent when over two hundred thousand seats were eliminated from race tracks because they could not be filled. The largest removal came at Talladega Speedway where over thirty thousand seats were eliminated. The decline in fans continued over the next seven years. The loss of fans spilled over into race teams and sponsorships. By 2017 Nascar teams were receiving over fifty percent less from sponsors than fifteen years prior. Long time sponsors Nextel, Monster Energy Drinks, Lowe's Home and Garden, and Target were just a few of the major sponsors lost. When asked about the decision all of the sponsors gave the same reasons, the cost of sponsorship had increased. The number of fans attending races and watching on television had decreased dramatically and the sponsors believed their advertising dollars could be better spent. Target put all of their "racing" money into soccer in the United States. Despite numerous rule changes, including adding the playoff system the number of fans attending races was so bad that Nascar quit providing race attendance figures in 2012 trying to silence the critics. All tracks suffered the same even Daytona. Daytona was the initial race ever run and was always the most popular and most attended race. During its hay day in 1998 Daytona sold two hundred thousand tickets and in 2018 they sold less than sixty thousand. The television viewers were also cut in half. When fans were asked why they quit attending races there was varying answers. These included the fact that there were no super star faces of racing. Many times, fans didn't even know most of the driver's names. In the past there were star drivers that fans either loved or despised, there was "Fireball" Roberts in the fifties, Richard Petty, David Pearson, the Yarborough brothers in the sixties and seventies, Dale Earnhardt and Cale Yarborough in the eighties. Later there was Dale Earnhardt Jr., Jeff Gordon, Jimmie Johnson, and Tony Stewart, then there was...there was...there was...well you get it, there was no star power. Another reason fans gave for the decline was the cost of attending the races had increased greatly over the years. In 2010 the average Daytona ticket cost a hundred and seventy dollars, by 2020 the average was nearly three hundred dollars. In 2018 the demise of Nascar racing hit an all-time low when Nascar owner and CEO Brian France put Nascar up for sale. Nascar was founded by Bill France Sr. in 1948. Later in 2018 France Jr. was arrested on DUI and drug charges. The consensus among Americans was that if you'd done to Nascar what he had, you'd be drinking and using drugs too. By 2020 things only got worse. In ten years from 2008-2018 Nascar dropped from ninety drivers and forty five operating teams to seventy drivers and less than twenty operating teams. By 2020 Daytona's attendance fell to forty five thousand and Nascar lost every major sponsor. The sport was also down to thirty drivers and fourteen operating teams. In contrast, short track racing in the South was at an all-time high. Fans waited in line Friday and Saturday nights all across the South to do what they used to do years earlier for Nascar. They came to the race, brought their own food and beverage and just had a good time without spending a fortune. The drivers? The only sponsors they had were themselves and maybe a buddy that owned a business would chip in a hundred bucks to have their business logo on the car. The best way I can put it is, it wasn't a case of Americans falling out of love with the sport. It was more a case of Nascar forgetting where it came from and in return where it came from forgot about Nascar. If Nascar management thought things couldn't get any worse, they were in for a big surprise. In 2020 with Covid -19 leaving Nascar races void of fans, the big joke was "well it doesn't look any different than the past five years" in reference to the already steep decline in nascar interest and attendance. 2020 was the first year that there was no sponsor of Nascar Racing. 2020 was also the year that the Black Lives Movement took America by storm. There were riots, protests, looting, and walkouts. There were cities that defunded police. Anything that had to do with slavery, slave owners, the Civil war or its hero's became the object of disgust. What did this have to do with the further decline of nascar? The rebel flag for decades had been a staple at every nascar race ever held. Now it was being barred from racetracks and so the only true fans left the so called "fifty-year-old rednecks" were further distanced from the sport they all once loved. On the other hand, things were really out of control. In July 2020 there was a "noose" found in the garage area of Nascar's only African American driver Bubba Wallace. This created a huge investigation that included the Federal Bureau of Investigation investigating it as a hate crime. The truth was that the rope had been used as a motor holder years prior. By 2022 there were only twenty drivers and ten operating teams. Sponsorship continued to decline and by 2022 many teams depended on numerous sponsors with no true sponsor. For thirty two years from 1971-2003 Nascar was sponsored by R.J. Reynolds tobacco company and was known as Winston Cup in reference to the popular Winston cigarette. From 2004-2007 Nextel became the sponsor. When Sprint bought Nextel, the name was changed to the Sprint Cup Series and they remained sponsors from 2008-2016. From 2017-2019 Monster Energy Drink sponsored the Nascar series. After forty nine years of major sponsorship Nascar was now faced with making it on small sponsorships with declining ticket revenue, declining television revenue, and a decline of interest. By the time 2022 rolled around the Covid-19 Pandemic, the rebel flag issues, and the further decline in sponsorship brought about a mass exodus of drivers. Many of the drivers could make a better living running the now popular Friday, Saturday, Sunday races at small tracks all over the south. Race tracks tried to find other uses to increase revenues. These included Christmas lights during the holidays, bike races, concerts, UFC fights, anything to make ends meet. Many of the tracks that no longer hosted races were destroyed. Most of the others eliminated seating. In 2023 Nascar's ten-year television deals with NBC Sports and Fox network worth over five and a half billion dollars expired. NBC and Fox both declined to even negotiate a deal to continue broadcasting. Nascar attorneys contacted every major network to gauge interest in broadcasting rights. There were no takers. In 1960 the first Nascar race was televised. Sixty three years later there would be no national coverage of nascar racing. Local networks scurried to secure television rights. Nascar had no choice but to agree at an all-time record low of five million dollars for one year. Even the local networks were not willing to extend the contract for more than one year without seeing some increase in ticket sales and interest in the sport. In 2024 Nascar reduced its normal thirty seven race schedule for the third consecutive year to an all-time low of twenty races. Daytona would be the season opener and the season would still begin in February. Daytona would also receive the final race of the season on July 4th to determine the Nascar Champion. Atlanta, Ga., Martinsville VA, Bristol Tn., Charlotte NC, Richmond Va., Talladega, Al., Kentucky, and Darlington SC with each track receiving two races. It appeared that Nascar was attempting to return to its roots keeping all of its races in the south where Nascar began. The season did not go well as attendance dropped below 20,000 per race. At the midway point of the season three teams filed for bankruptcy leaving only seven teams and fifteen drivers to compete. On the eve of the final race July 4, 2024 the France family called a news conference. The news conference was sparsely attended as only eighteen thousand fans were in attendance for the championship race. There were reporters from every major network and numerous media representatives but about five hundred media people short of what a major announcement from Nascar would have drawn decades earlier. As attorneys and representatives of Nascar entered the ballroom of the hotel everyone noted how empty the room was. The only speaker would be the official attorney of Nascar. " I thank each of you for attending today's announcement. This is a day we have all tried to avoid for many years now. For many years Nascar was one of the most popular sports in America. Today we are here to announce that Nascar racing will be ceasing all operations and will be filing for bankruptcy effective tomorrow. Tomorrows race has been officially cancelled. We will be closing our doors after seventy six years of fan pleasing bumper to bumper racing. There are many reason for the decline we have witnessed leading to this decision. The decrease in popularity of all sports, the Covid-19 scare, the racial issues, and the lack of financial stability all led to the decline in attendance, sponsorships, television revenue, concessions, and memorability leading to today's sad announcement. Thus, the end of Nascar on July 4, 2024.

# Chapter VIII

A ttorney Shaun O'Leary closed the book and remembered the day he'd heard the announcement concerning the end of Nascar racing. Now he believed that Nascar was the victim of its own greed that included nationwide expansion, closing the popular smaller tracks, and enormous sponsor fees. When a company spends 35 million dollars to sponsor a race car, their better be fans in the stands and millions more watching on television to see their logo 500 times as the car circles the track. Otherwise the advertising funds could be spent in a much smarter fashion. Shaun knew he'd also need sponsors for a new league, new teams would need sponsors. He felt like baseball would be a much easier "pitch" than any of the other sports. He knew ESPN would be on board as they struggled with coverage limited to bowling, golf, and of course soccer which netted eighty percent of their entertainment. They would surely receive the return of professional baseball with open arms. O'Leary spent the next month writing emails, making phone calls, attending meetings, and promoting his idea. He hired a staff of 20 professionals, all assigned to different task. He rented yet another floor in the high-rise office building that housed his thriving law firm. On the office doors and on the entrance lobby sign were the words "OPERATION BRING BACK BASEBALL. He now looked forward to Rocket Beal's next article and reading the next chapter of "The Demise".

O'Leary had anticipated the series of New York News articles by Rocket Beal because he saw this as an opportunity to learn the aspects of sports history he'd missed. Despite being born into a wealthy family and becoming a billionaire at an early age, he respected his elders and felt like everyone could learn from them and the experience and wisdom they'd obtained over the years. He was very interested in the articles because he knew that Beal would be honest, forthcoming, and totally brutal if necessary. He also knew that he and some of his wealthy business partners had enough financial resources to rescue sports or at least try to bring something back that Americans would love besides soccer. Despite being financially involved, soccer just wasn't his thing. For years now instead of watching baseball during the dog days of summer and anticipating the World Series in October, he watched golf and tennis. Not quite as exciting. Instead of looking forward to NFL football in September and preparing for his family's annual Super Bowl party in January, he was forced to watch indoor soccer or professional bowling. Friends just didn't have annual bowling championship parties. He missed those Super Bowl parties. The thing the attorney missed most was the loss of NCAA college sports and in particular NCAA basketballs March Madness. No more madness and no more brackets to fill out. At this point he was left looking forward to the National Futbol League games that spanned from May through the Super Bowl of Futbol in September. He was not the only one that missed all of the old sports, most Americans missed them. Yes, the fans lack of interest contributed to the downfall in some sports like Nascar, the National Basketball Association, and Major League baseball. They however were not to blamed for the downfall of the NFL or NCAA sports. Shaun O'Leary was now more determined than ever to bring back America's sport, Major League baseball. He felt like baseball was Americas game and its favorite sport. Despite being founded first, it ended last. The attorney felt that baseballs demise was because it was expanded too much while signing too many television and media contracts. Baseball owners depended on the contracts to pay the bills that included the stadium, players and staff salaries, and all the things that owners were financially responsible for. They failed to calculate that the fans would take advantage of the televised games and that this would keep them away from the stadiums so they traded the television contracts for the fans. Television contracts don't buy concessions or apparel or pay for parking. O'Leary remembered hearing his family talk about when there were only two leagues, there was only one televised game per week on Saturday afternoon. This forced the fans to attend the games in person if they wanted to see them. During the sixties and before there were twenty major league regular season games televised per year. By 2020 there was over eight hundred games televised per season. This didn't include the baseball channel that televised all twenty four hundred games a season for less than a hundred dollars. So, for the cost of four upper deck tickets to one game, a fan could watch every single game in a season on television. Then they could watch all of the playoff games and World Series games for free. Why would fans go to games? It seemed obvious to O'Leary that with proper management baseball could be the first American professional sport to revive and become more popular than ever. He knew that America was craving something besides soccer or "futbol".

Twenty miles away Floyd and Manna sat together and worked on the next article. While Manna was no fan of sports she tried to keep up with as much as she could so she'd have something to talk to Beal about. She also knew without her help he'd never be able to meet the deadlines for the articles. He couldn't even remember when the deadlines were. So together they finished the article after eight pain staking hours. The following day she planned to read it to him and see how much he remembered about it.

# Chapter IX

Floyd Beal sat down at the kitchen table and started to eat his oatmeal that Manna prepared for him every morning. It wasn't oatmeal with any brown sugar and cinnamon or apples and raisins. Nope Beal only ate his with butter and salt. Like eating popcorn at the drive in theatre he'd say. Manna picked up the morning paper and said she was going to read him the article. "Hell no Manna, give me that paper. You think I can't read anymore?" She wanted to tell him some days he could and some days he couldn't but she kept that thought to herself. Beal began reading his article with Manna looking over his shoulder.:

The decade from the sixties to the seventies was one of the most historic in all of history. I'm not just talking in the world of sports but in the world itself. The Vietnam war was a daily topic during this decade and for decades to come. I don't think anybody actually knows why we were there and what even happened. I know this for sure, there was no winners and many lives were lost. In other politics, the first ever presidential debate was held between John F. Kennedy and Richard Nixon. Kennedy would win the debate and the election before being assassinated by Lee Harvey Oswald on November 22, 1963. The shots that killed President Kennedy were heard around the world and his death was mourned for years to come. Everybody remembered exactly where they were and what they were doing "the day President Kennedy was assassinated". In 1965 another event that still effects American citizens today was the creation of Medicare helping the elderly pay for healthcare after age sixty five. 1960 witnessed the availability of "birth control" pills to married women only and by 1965 there were over five million women using the pills. Many believe that "the pill" was partly responsible for the sexual revolution. In 1963 the world was shocked to learn of the first heart transplant. On July 20, 1969 Apollo Eleven landed on the moon and Neil Armstrong became the first human to step foot on the lunar surface, placing an American flag on the surface. Over half a billion people tuned in to watch the event unfold. Two months later over four hundred thousand people called "hippies", a name coined by a San Francisco Examiner writer in 1965, converged in Bethel New York for a three-day music festival known as Woodstock. There were less than two hundred thousand tickets sold but over four hundred thousand attended and despite all the obstacles, all those hippies were able to have a three-day concert with no violence. Woodstock is still the largest and most talked about outdoor music festival in history. During the decade the first email was sent in 1969 between colleges UCLA and Stanford University. The Civil rights movement was in full swing and there seemed to be news daily about protest all over the country from individuals and groups. On August 28, 1963 Dr. Martin Luther King gave the now famous "I have a dream speech" standing in front of the Lincoln Memorial in Washington DC with over a quarter million in attendance. Less than a year later the Civil Rights act was passed. Three months later Dr. King was awarded the Nobel Peace Prize. Sadly, four years later Dr. King was assassinated in Memphis Tennessee. It's easy to see how much changed in all aspects of life from 1960-1970 and the world of sports was no different. There were many firsts along the way.

In Major League baseball Bill Mazeroski became the 1st player to end a World Series with a home run in 1960 leading the Pittsburg Pirates to the title in seven games. Seventy years later the feat has not been duplicated and the film of that event is played somewhere daily.

As for the National Basketball Association there were also many historical events that still stand out today. On March 1, 1962 Wilt Chamberlin became the first professional player to score a hundred points in a game. That record still stands today. Another NBA record that still stands is the Boston Celtics winning eight straight NBA titles from 1958-1966. They eventually won nine of the ten titles during the 1960's. That would never happen again thanks to free agency.

The National Football League's biggest news of the decade was the playing of the first Super Bowl between the NFL's Green Bay Packers coached by the great Hall of Fame coach Vince Lombardi and the Kansas City Chiefs. The game matched the NFL Champion and the American Football League (AFL) champion for the first time in history. The Packers won the first Super Bowl and would win Super Bowl II the following season defeating the Oakland Raiders. Until the playing of Super Bowl I, the two leagues teams never played against each other but were fierce rivals when it came to competing for fans and revenue. Both leagues believed they had the better teams, fans, and stadiums. In 1966 when the National Football League and the American Football League agreed to merge using the NFL name and logo, there was still many details before the merger was complete. The merger became final in 1970 and after many years the two leagues teams became regular season foes on the field.

In college sports the UCLA Bruins basketball team won the first of a record seven consecutive titles in 1967, a record nobody has come close to in the seventy three years since then. Two in a row is the best anybody has done and that feat has only been duplicated twice since. The Bruins would actually go on to win ten titles in twelve seasons and at one point had a record eighty eight-game winning streak. The Bruins were coached by the legendary John Wooden, the greatest college coach of all time. He was also the inventor of the Pyramid of Success (look it up, it'll do you good).

While college basketball was being dominated by the Bruins, college football was not being dominated at all. In fact, they couldn't even pick one national champion. Only Darrell Royals 1963 Texas Longhorns were crowned unanimous National Champions. Some years during the decade there were as many as five voted National Champions. This was because there were so many polls and rankings that declared the national champion. Despite the fact that there were thirty national champions during the decade, Ohio State and Alabama each snagged four apiece, Notre Dame and Texas followed with three, and so the four schools combined for half of the thirty national titles won.

Boxing had been a huge success for many decades and its popularity was right up there with the other professional sports in popularity. During the sixties however, the prize fights no longer had to be listened to on the radio, they could now be watched on black and white TV for those that could afford one. Those that couldn't either ask a neighbor to watch or stood in front of a Sears and watched through the storefront window. While the previous decade was dominated by a host of great fighters including Rocket Marciano, Joe Louis, and Floyd Patterson, it was one boxer that dominated the 1960's all by himself. This boxer was Cassias Clay, who would later change his name to Muhammad Ali. The world had never seen a cockier, more brash, more flamboyant boxer and people either adored the man or despised him. In 1964 the then Clay "shocked the world" by winning the World Heavyweight title with a seventh-round knockout of then champion Sonny Liston. He would fight his last fight of the decade in 1967 as his refusal to enter the Vietnam war time draft caused him to be convicted of "draft dodging". He claimed he was Muslim and his beliefs made it impossible for him to kill. He could beat your ass up in a fight but not kill you. After being stripped of his titles and arrested he was finally found innocent by the Supreme Court and allowed to continue his boxing career the following decade.

Soccer in the decade was just starting to take off and gain in popularity in the 1960's. In 1959 the NCAA starting to sanction men's soccer at the college level and held its first national championship. This led to many universities starting soccer programs. The first two professional soccer leagues were created in 1967. The United Soccer Association and National Professional Soccer League. The two merged in 1968 to form the North American Soccer League. There's nobody that would have believed that eventually the North American Soccer League would later become the National Futbol League and become one of the most popular sports leagues in the world.

Professional wrestling continued its rise in popularity all over the United States with its "hero" and "villain" actors. Golf and tennis continued to remain steady on the professional fronts and both gained popularity as casual weekend sports.

There was much to like about sports in the sixties, with many first, many records broken that still stand, various dominate performances, but the most amazing thing was the lack of controversy. There was also no decline in popularity of the sports so the sixties may have been one of the most memorable and best decades ever for sports and its fans in the United States. "

At almost the exact same time Beal read his article Shaun O'Leary was opening his laptop to see what Beal had to say. After finishing the article O'Leary said out loud "What another great article"! O' Leary also thought about what a wonderful decade of sports the sixties must have been without all of the troubles that would soon follow. If there was anything to learn from this article it was how positive things could actually be if things were done the right way. That's exactly what he planned to do, do things the right way!

Forty miles away but worlds apart Joe Mills read the second article and couldn't believe how well his friend was progressing with the articles despite his diagnosis. Joe dropped what he was doing and called his old friend. Manna answered the phone and told him that Floyd was napping. She told him "it seems like doing the second article has exhausted him. Its either that or the four shots of Shine. That was what Beal referred to his Tennessee moonshine as. Yea that was probably it, Joe thought. It was a drink he had never tasted and had no interest in doing so. The only thing he knew about moonshine was that Granny on the television show the Beverly Hillbillies drank it and smoke came out of her ears. Joe hung up the phone and went outside to sit on his white swing. He and Bea had been planning for years to spend a lot of time in that swing but his work always seemed to get in the way. They hadn't even been on a vacation in over twelve years. The last time they had, it was to Hawaii for Joe to cover the NFL Pro Bowl. Not much of a vacation. One day...he thought, one day he'd fulfill that promise to Bea.

# Chapter X

eading up to the next of Beal's article two weeks later O'Leary continued to work with a number of other attorneys on the NCAA case. Any extra time he had was spent on preparing for the upcoming meetings for the All-American Baseball League. Shaun's wife Cindy was starting to complain about not seeing him at all. He had never been at home much because his profession carried him all over the country but recently he was around even less. He'd promised her that as soon as he got the new league off the ground he'd have time for the family. She wasn't so sure about that. "What'll it be next? A new basketball league? " Not a bad idea he thought but he'd have never said that to her. Well not today anyway.

Joe Mills called his friend again a few days before the third article. Floyd told him this was a tough one to write. Once you start writing about that decade you start to realize innocence was lost in our country itself and in the world of sports. While the 1960's were calm, cool, and collected, the seventies were anything but that. Joe understood and was anticipating the article. So far, so good he thought. The following day the article would be published. Floyd would be one step closer to being finished with the project. Mills was starting to feel bad for asking his friend to take on such a large project in his condition. Joe hadn't realized that Floyd's disease was so advanced. He also knew it was a project that Manna had not volunteered for. It was too late to worry about now so he just looked forward to seeing what his friend had to say the next day. The next morning he awoke to the smell of bacon cooking. He thought to himself "who could ever sleep through the smell of bacon cooking"? Not him for sure. He got out of bed and went straight to his office where Bea already had his coffee waiting. She knew he'd go straight to his office, open his laptop, and read Floyd Beal's next special article. He opened his laptop and noticed the lead story was about Shaun O'Leary winning a motion in the Supreme Court case in his attempt to bring back college sports. He was really interested in the article but it'd have to wait. He started reading his friends article:

By the time the seventies rolled around I was twenty years old and playing college baseball at Tennessee University. I loved all sports but baseball was the one I excelled at and the one that afforded me the opportunity to attend college. I guess you could call an estimated hundred mile per hour fastball excelling. I remember a lot about the times because boy were they changing rapidly, not only in sports but in every aspect of life. There were many monumental and historic events that changed the world during this decade. The most popular "rock and roll" band in history, the Beatles, broke up in 1970 after eleven successful years. They originated in 1960 in Liverpool England and took America by storm two years later in what would later be coined the British Invasion. They not only had sales of over eight hundred million albums worldwide but also made numerous movies and television appearances. Along the same musical line, America's Top Forty radio program became the first syndicated weekly radio show in history. The weekly show ranked the top forty rock and roll songs each week and Casey Kasem played them all counting them down from number forty to number one.

The decade was also much more politically motivated. In May 1970 four students from Kent State University were killed and nine others injured when the Ohio National Guard opened fire on protesters protesting the Vietnam war. This incident led to national changes that still exist when dealing with authorities and demonstrators. In 1971 there was a permanent ban put on tobacco advertising on television and radio. That sure didn't help curb smoking. The number of smokers only continued to increase rapidly until 1975. The Watergate hotel scandal rocked the nation and resulted in the arrest of more than sixty people and the resignation of President Richard M. Nixon the nations thirty seventh President.

1976 was huge for the United States as everyone celebrated the 200th Anniversary of our nation. That same year major league baseball celebrated its one hundred thirty seventh birthday, professional football celebrated its hundred and eighth birthday, professional basketball celebrated just its thirtieth year and Nascar its twenty eighth year.

College and professional sports continued to flourish in the 1970's. While there were many great inspiring stories during the decade there were also quite a few disasters involving sports and teams that the nation had never witnessed in prior decades. In a six-week span in the fall of 1970 the Wichita State football team and the Marshall University football team were involved in plane crashes that took over a hundred lives. Seven years later in 1977, the Evansville men's basketball team was involved in a crash that killed twenty nine people including the entire team and coaching staff. To date there has never been another disaster involving college or professional teams.

Although this was still a time of love, peace, happiness, and rock and roll, there were still sporting scandals. Among those, the International Olympic Committee was forced to introduce drug testing of the athletes at the 1972 Munich Olympics due to wide spread cheating in the previous decade. Seven athletes were disqualified. In 1975 Anabolic Steroids was added to banned substances. At the time nobody could have known that steroids would change the entire history of sports. In 1978-79 underworld figures, that would be the mafia to you and me, paid Boston College basketball players to fix the outcomes of games allowing them to rake in millions of gambling winnings, and the list could go on and on but you get the picture. Evil was easing its way into the world and the world of sports.

As far as the conditions and outlooks of the individual sports leagues, each was having its own negative issues or successes.

Major League Baseball continued its popularity but not because of the parity the league had hoped for. In fact, it was just the opposite. The decade was dominated by six teams. Those six teams accounted for eighteen of the twenty World Series participants during the 70's. Three teams, the Oakland A's, Cincinnati Reds, and the New York Yankees all won back to back World Series. Television contributed to the growth and popularity of MLB. By 1970 major league baseball had grown to twenty four teams. Television revenues had jumped to a gross of almost twenty one million dollars. In comparison twenty years earlier in 1950 there were sixteen teams and only two million dollars in television revenue. In 1975 professional baseball games expanded from once a week televised games on Saturday afternoons by adding a Monday night game. NBC paid seventy two million dollars to televise Monday night games for three seasons. By 1975 baseball was at the height of its popularity and once again became America's game. By 1976 the three major networks NBC, ABC and CBS were all broadcasting baseball to the tune of ninety eight million dollars for three years. Attendance grew during the decade increasing from twenty nine million in 1970 to over forty three million in 1979.

The NFL also flourished in the 1970's much in part to newly negotiated television contracts with all three major networks. In the late 70's the Louis Harris sports survey indicated that seventy percent of Americans followed the NFL while MLB had a following of only fifty four percent. The NFL was also voted Americas favorite sport by a ten percent margin. followed by Major League baseball. The NFL experimented with expanding its product by playing its first game in Mexico in 1978. In 1978 attendance exceeded twelve million for the first time in history averaging over fifty three thousand fans per game. During the seventy's safety became a major topic and many new rules were introduced to improve the safety of the players. Little did they realize that the one safety measure that mattered most, concussions, was being overlooked, ignored and marginalized.

While the NBA was having its own issues there were also some success stories. The NBA added two teams to increase the league to nineteen teams. In the mid-seventies the league went over four hundred thousand in attendance for the first time, an average of fifteen thousand per game. On the court parity was the theme of the decade. Following the Boston Celtics winning ten titles in eleven years in the previous decades, the seventies saw eight different teams crowned champion.

The NCAA major sports (Football and Men's basketball) during the 70's brought about rollercoaster numbers as far as attendance in both football and men's basketball. In 1970 the average attendance for an NCAA football game was thirty two thousand per game. This would be the highest average of the decade. The second highest was in 1979 with an average of twenty five thousand per game. Men's basketball attendance for Division 1 schools averaged forty eight hundred fans per game in 1976. By the end of the decade the average had increased to over six thousand per game. Television played no part on the success of college basketball in the early 70's. During those early years only seven NCAA tournament games would be televised. Fifty years later all one hundred and twenty eight games were televised. The number of NCAA tournament games that were televised increased every year from 1973 until 1979. This television exposure helped increase the revenue that assisted in paying for all of the other sports.

Soccer in the 1970's was just starting to gain popularity in America. The decade included the origination and the eventual demise of the MLS (Major League Soccer). The league was popular early on but grew too fast. That combined with the disappointment of not getting the World Cup nod to host the games damaged the growth potential. Thanks to the passage of title IX women's college soccer teams grew to be more than a hundred. Soccer started becoming more prevalent on the youth and high school scenes.

Men's and women's professional tennis, and golf continued to thrive. Professional wrestling and roller derby skating continued to maintain active fan bases despite the fact that the results and the fights were scripted. But....you better not tell a wrestling or roller derby fan that or you'd have an unscripted fight on your hands.

Summing up the decade known as the 1970's would be hard to do. There was a lot of growth due to television contracts. A lot of great teams and a lot of great players entertained us during the decade. While the 1970's saw great success, the road to success would become a little rockier in the 1980's. More about that in my next article".

Joe finished the article and thought to himself that this was Beal's best article yet. Maybe the new mushroom concoction that Manna was sneaking in his morning coffee was helping him. After finishing the article Mills turned his attention to the story about attorney O'Leary's small victory in the Supreme Court case. The court voted to allow O'Leary access to financial and attendance documents from college sports from the past ten years. He has a chance Mills thought.

Attorney Shaun O'Leary finished reading the article about his victory and then read Floyd Beal's newest article. He was happy to be home for an evening with Cindy. He was never home early. This was the first time in months he'd been home before dark. She'd made his favorite Irish stew to celebrate his small victory. After dinner they played a game of Scrabble which was always a favorite of the family. Later that evening he'd found time to read article number three for a second time. He originally read the articles as a means to help his new league succeed. He soon realized just how much he enjoyed the history of not only sports but what was going on around Beal during those times. After finishing the article O'Leary was beginning to see how sports had evolved over time. He had always understood the business end of professional sports but reading the articles and Joe Mill's book The Demise opened his mind to all of the other things that contributed to the rise and then the fall of professional sports. Things like politics and the government. This was never truer than the suspension of all NCAA college sports. The suspension was now in its fourth year and was now in the hands of the Supreme Court. O'Leary wondered how could a group of women bring down something as powerful of an institution as the National

Collegiate Athletic Association and negatively affect so many others. It seemed pretty selfish to him. Maybe he'd learn more about the details from the next chapter of The Demise. He lit a cigar, Cindy brought him a glass of wine and once again reminded him of the scrabble beating he'd endured earlier in the evening. He opened the book.

# Chapter XI

S haun O'Leary had always wondered exactly how a group of women or any other group were able to bring an abrupt end to college sports effecting nearly a half million student athletes. He would soon learn how it was possible when he took on the case. Although he was probably more informed on the topic than anyone else he was very interested in Joe Mills take on the situation. The next chapter was titled "Equal Rights or Bust"! Joe Mills had written:

The NCAA or National Collegiate Athletic Association was founded in 1910. Originally it was a discussion and rulemaking group. In 1921 the first NCAA championship was held. Oddly enough the first championship was in track and field. Gradually more rules were created and more sports were included as NCAA championships. The first college basketball tournament was held in 1939. That tournament would eventually become known as March Madness and would generate more than seven hundred million dollars annually until the suspension of all collegiate sports in 2026. By 1952 there were more teams, more sports to be governed, college football bowl games were increasing every year and the NCAA became a crucial part of college sports. In 1951 the NCAA named its first director and by 1952 had opened its first offices in Kansas City, Missouri. It wasn't until the 1980's that the NCAA adopted women sports. Prior to that women college sports were governed by the AIAW or Association for Intercollegiate Athletics for women. Forty years later the NCAA would sorely regret the addition. It wouldn't take long for the women to become problematic. In 1999 the NCAA was sued for not providing as many sports for women as they did for men. Colleges also did not spend as much money on women sports and despite having logical financial reasoning, the lawsuit was allowed to proceed under Title IX (Nine). The suit moved all the way to the Supreme Court. Without going into the legal jargon and to put it in Layman's terms each college would be forced to spend as much money and offer as many sports for women as it did for men. The number of women compared to the number of men at each college would be used to determine athletic teams and finances dedicated to each. Two decades later this same law would once again raise its ugly head and the results were the suspension of all NCAA sports. Prior to 2026 college athletics were already suffering. In the Dark Year 2020, eighty-four sports were terminated from thirty-five different universities. Trying not to violate Title Nine laws only nine of the eighty-four were women's teams. By 2025 another one hundred and forty sports had been eliminated including thirty-eight football teams. I think now is a good time to get on my high horse or my soap box as my mother called it. First you have to realize that in 2019 there were ninety different NCAA sports, forty-six women and forty-one men. Only five sports were actually profitable and more than paid for itself. Those five included a few surprises. The first was not a surprise, NCAA Men's basketball generated over nine hundred thousand dollars per year. That money was funneled to fourteen different entities from Academic Enhancement Funds and Educational Support to athletic scholarships. The other four sports that were self-supporting were Men's Ice Hockey, Men's Lacrosse, Men's baseball and Men's Wrestling. It's fair to say that without men's basketball there would be very few sports that could survive on their own. If you take a look at the profitable sports you'll notice five things, men's, men's, men's, men's, and men's. Yes, all five are men's sports. This means that not a single women's college sport supported itself. Not one. What really got the gender discrimination lawsuit initiated in 2026 all began, once again in March of that dark year 2020. The US Women's National Soccer team filed a lawsuit against the U.S. Soccer Federation. The lawsuit was intended to provide the much more successful women's team players the same pay as the Men's National team. The reason I bring this up while writing about NCAA sports is because of the court ruling in the Women's National Team lawsuit and the court's reasoning as it parallels the NCAA case currently in the Supreme Courts hands. How so?

There were twenty eight players that were part of the suit alleging that the United States Soccer Association engages in "institutionalized gender discrimination" toward the team. The discrimination "has caused, contributed to, and perpetuated gender-based pay disparities" against the players in "nearly every aspect of their employment," the lawsuit read. The lawsuit was filed in U.S. District Court for the Central District of California under the Equal Pay Act and Title VII of the Civil Rights Act. The USSA countered with two arguments. First, they presented evidence that the women team players were paid equal to the men. Second, they presented evidence that showed the U.S. Men's team generated much more revenue than the women's team. In a study by the Wall Street Journal it was revealed that from 2014- 2018 men's games generated nineteen million more dollars than the women's team. In May 2020 a judge dismissed the equal pay portion of the lawsuit. Now back to the NCAA. Why should women teams be given the same importance and financial support when not a single one generates enough revenue to support itself? If not for men's basketball they'd have no sports at all. That didn't matter to a group of former USNWT players, WNBA players, and over a hundred female student athletes that formed the class action group Operation Equality. The women were upset that from 2019-2025 more than half of women sports had been eliminated by colleges due to financial hardships. The courts agreed and in early 2026 an order halting all college sports was issued until a formal and final decision could be rendered. The order shocked every sports fan in America. It also shocked student athletes across America. If there were no tickets sold, no NCAA basketball tournament, no football bowl games, who would pay for athletic scholarships? The first year there was enough savings to cover the cost. Entering the second year of the suspension of sports, all recruiting ceased, coaches were furloughed, and student athletes were informed that the universities could no longer carry the burden of the cost of the scholarships. These actions caused a firestorm like no other. There were massive protest on every campus in America. Lawsuits were filed all across the country. Baseball, basketball and soccer players flocked overseas or turned professional in order to continue their athletic careers. I personally believe that this is one of the worst cases of injustice that I have ever witnessed. I'm not talking about the so-called injustice Operation Equality claims. I'm talking about the injustice suffered by all those student athletes and their families s at the hands of Operation Equality. As we enter another fall without college football, I wonder if the courts will ever make a decision so college sports can resume. If the court rules in favor of Operation Equality, there will be no possible way for colleges to support men and women teams equally. It's just not financially feasible. If the court rules against Operation Equality, women will feel like they have been forced to take a step back in the never-ending fight for equality. So how do we fix this? It's simple and it's a plan where everyone wins, well almost everyone. So, who loses? Fencers, swimmers, golfers, cross country runners, gymnast, rifle shooters, rowers, divers, and water polo players because these sports would be completely eliminated from college sports. Take a minute and think about the savings on facilities, travel, equipment, uniforms, coaches' salaries, and the list goes on and on. Hey I'm not picking on anyone or any sport. but seriously how many people attend those sporting events? The parents, the friends, and the grandparents? By eliminating these sports, the men's basketball program alone could more than support the remaining sports. So what sports do we keep making it equal for both men and women. Men's sports would include football, basketball, baseball, soccer, lacrosse, track and field, and hockey. Women's sports would include basketball, soccer, softball, volleyball, lacrosse, track and field, and field hockey. That's seven sports each for the men and seven for the women. How did I come up with which sports to eliminate? That also is simple. Eliminate the ones that are only on ESPN on replay after midnight and the ones nobody attends except parents and friends...and, so you get the point. The remaining sports are the most popular, most watched, and most financially self-supporting. Simplicity is underestimated. Now all we do is wait.

O'Leary closed The Demise and thought Mills idea's for resurrecting NCAA sports were excellent. No wonder this was a Pulitzer Prize winning book. The ideas were simple yes but had the potential to solve a problem effecting nearly half a million student athletes, coaches, and universities nationwide. O'Leary started thinking about why and when he had decided to file a lawsuit demanding an injunction until the high court's made a decision, allowing college sports to resume. He'd thought that maybe that would push the Supreme Court to come to a decision. All of a sudden, he was shocked back into reality. He had to quit worrying about college athletics right now, he had a professional baseball league to launch. He laughed when he thought how odd it was that his ideas for the new league were also simple. Maybe simplicity was the key to success. Maybe it was time for O'Leary to finally meet Joseph J. Mills. It was simple as that.

# Chapter XII

By the time Rocket Beal's 3rd article was published O'Leary had made great strides in a short period of time in his quest to revive professional baseball in America. By April first, his "Super Team" as he liked to refer to them were starting to show why they were picked for their individual tasks because of their individual strengths and talents. On October first there would be the first meeting of the Super Team minds. This meeting was a chance for each expert to give an update on their assignments. There was a need for this meeting as the first board of directors and owners meeting would be held a week later followed by a national news conference. As Coach O'Leary, as the team referred to him, entered the huge boardroom he was given a standing ovation. O'Leary laughed and started the meeting by saying "I hope all of you still feel the same way about me three months from now." It was time to get to work. The meeting started promptly at eight o'clock that morning. First to present was the attorney husband and wife team of McGovern and McGovern. They were old friends of O'Leary's family and he knew they were two of the most organized professionals he'd ever met. He also knew that Paul McGovern was a huge sports fans and they had attended many sporting events together in years past. Paul's presentation was entitled "The League". "My name is Paul McGovern. My wife Sarah and I are honored to be asked by coach O'Leary to join his team. Our goal from day one has been to see his goal to a successful fruition. Our first task was to form the league which we have successfully done. The league will be called The American Baseball League or ABL for short. The logo was designed exclusively for the league by professional sports artists from all over America. I am happy to unveil for you the American Baseball League logo. " He then dropped the cover to unveil an amazing eye catching red, white, and blue logo that included a waving American flag flying above a red, white and blue map of the United States . The room exploded with, clapping, high fiving and everyone there happy to have something that now identified what they were working on. Paul continued " All trademarks have been obtained. All rights have been obtained and most importantly Coach O'Leary has approved the name and logo after six previous failures." Paul set down. Next to approach the podium was the former Commissioner of Major League baseball Frank Beamer. He'd been hired by O'Leary to recruit potential cities and owners for teams and potential board members that would help direct the league. Who would be more qualified to recruit potential owners and board members than the person who'd worked with them during the most difficult times of Major League Baseball. "Good morning to you all" he started. " I'll have to say my job was much easier than I ever anticipated and I have great news. I have attracted twelve cities with stadiums, twelve owners willing to pay two million dollars for a team and run the team within the new rules adopted by the league. We actually had twenty owners and cities wanting to join the league but we negotiated with our top potential owners and with input from coach O'Leary selected what we felt were the twelve strongest applicants. We then gave each owner time to select a team name and trademark it. As far as logos, team colors, etc. this will be completed in the near future." The first season is scheduled to kick off in 14 months with opening day to be held on Memorial Day 2031. "We also secured contracts that forbids any leaking of information or media notice prior to the meeting with owners, directors, and the national press conference. I'd now like to announce the selected cities that will make up the initial American Baseball League. In the Eastern League there will be the Boston Marathoners, New York Big Apples, New York Empires, Chicago Winds, Chicago Fire and the Cleveland Supermen . The Western League will consist of the Los Angeles Stars, Houston Energizers, California Redwoods, San Diego Farmers, Oakland Sea

Monsters, and the Texas Cowboys. It didn't surprise him that the new owners chose to change the names and mascots from the previous failed league as these were ways to make everything new and exciting. All logos were designed to fit the new names and the new times. The reason we were able to so easily persuade the current owners to step up was because they were so impressed with the outline for the league I presented to them. Now to explain to you how the league will work and what impressed the new owners is the team of Frank and Mike Riley." This father and son team wrote an editorial letter to several national newspapers with their ideas about how professional baseball could have been saved. O'Leary put a lot of stock in their opinions. After all, when you have a father and son team that both graduated from Oxford University, you tend to take notice. Both of the Riley's approached the podium. Frank would start " My son Mike and I were approached by Coach O'Leary after several editorials we wrote were printed outlining our combined ideas. We have listed these things in numerical order to make it easier for reference.

Number one- Only one television contract has been negotiated. It will include one televised game per week on Sunday afternoons. It will also include the seven game league championship series and the seven game American Series. These contracts will be negotiated by Coach O'Leary himself.

Number two- The teams will only play teams within its own league until the American Series. This will greatly decrease travel expenditures for each team.

Number three- Each team will play a sixty two-game schedule with the season beginning Memorial Day weekend and the American Series starting Labor Day weekend and concluding when the first team wins four games. Playoff and American Series games will also be played only on weekends.

Number four- Games will be scheduled for every Friday, Saturday, and Sunday. There is no preference as far as night games and day games.

There will also be double headers played every other Saturday. These double headers will consist of two seven inning games.

Number five- Ticket prices will all be set prices to coincide with the prices at every other stadium. Season tickets may be sold at a twenty five percent discount of the normal ticket price. Maximum ticket prices will be fifty dollars for the best seats and ten dollars for the worst. All others will fall somewhere in between.

Number six: Concession prices and memorabilia prices cannot exceed thirty three percent of the actual cost. An example is the common hot dog. If it cost the stadium two dollars for ingredients and add in the for labor and packaging, then they can charge five dollars for that hot dog, not twelve. We have to make this affordable for the average family. Over the next couple of months, we'll determine the prices for concessions based on pertinent facts. The same goes for parking. We will be offering free parking to our fans. Once again, we have to make this experience affordable for everyone.

Number seven: Player salaries will be capped at a total of two and a half million dollars. Players will be ranked and paid accordingly based on a sliding scale. The number one ranked player on the team receives five hundred thousand per season., Then it drops to seventy five thousand per year for players ranked twenty through twenty five. The team manager will receive a one hundred thousand dollar base and the three coaches will receive fifty thousand per season. The total team payroll excluding office staff will be three million dollars. The math is simple: A team spends three million dollars on player and coaches' salaries. They play thirty one home games and the average ticket price is thirty five dollars. They would only need twenty eight hundred paying fans per game to break even. The cost of the stadium, stadium employees, and incidentals would be covered by concessions, memorabilia and television income.

Number eight: Each team will consist of twenty five players.

Number nine: Profits from all playoff games and World Series will be divided equally between participating players and coaches.

Number ten: Television revenues will not be shared with players as these funds will be utilized for operational and promotion cost. Each owner will receive five percent of the television revenue.

The remaining presenters were concerned with safety, security, player acquisition, and advertising. O'Leary left the meeting at seven on the dot, exactly eleven hours after it began feeling like his dream was going to become a reality. His next step would be to prepare for the owners' meetings. Before meeting with the owners Shaun O'Leary hoped to finish "The Demise". He hoped that the facts and opinions surrounding the contents of the book would help him with his upcoming presentation presenting the model for constructing a successful professional league. Being an agent and a sports fan for his entire life, O'Leary had a pretty good idea and his own opinion as to what happened to professional sports in America. It wasn't until he started reading Mill's book that he saw things from a different point of view. Not only the view of a sports editor but that of a fan. He opened the book and started reading the next chapter.

# Chapter XIII

W ho caused the demise of the NBA I've often been asked. Was it the owners, the management, the players, the fans, the times? To be honest all of the above contributed to the ball being dropped and eventually deflating the league It wasn't one thing or one decade that attributed to the downfall of the National Basketball Association, it was a combination of many. The NBA was always a fragile league depending on superstars and super teams to fuel interest in the sport. As far back as the fifties the league struggled falling to eight teams after three teams folded during the decade. By the end of the decade the top drawing team was still attracting a mere six thousand fans per game through the turnstiles.

The sixties was certainly a two-way street for the game and the league. On one side of the street attendance continued to fall, television contracts were small and there was very little interest in the league. On the other side of the street the decade provided some of the best teams and players in NBA history. By the mid- sixties attendance increased to over two million. That sounds like a nice fat figure until you compare it to Major League Baseball drawing over ten times that number of fans. NBA games were televised once a week and attracted few fans because the fans were watching the NFL on Sundays, not the NBA. The night that Wilt Chamberlin scored a hundred points in a game there was no television coverage and only four thousand fans witnessed the feat that would never be repeated. While the Celtics of the sixties were fun to watch and were named the greatest team in history, their dominance actually hurt the game. When a team wins nine titles in ten years, it makes for a lot of boredom unless of course you were a Boston Celtic fan.

As if the league didn't have enough issues now there was a new more exciting game in town. The American Basketball Association was founded in 1967 and was fun. The league came up with fun ideas to gain fans interests. Fans had the ABA to thank for the three-point line, the dunk contest, and red white and blue basketballs. Former NBA star and first true "big man" George Mikan was named the first commissioner of the league. The ABA attracted stars that would have been NBA players including Julius "Doctor J" Erving, David Thompson and Connie Hawkins. Both leagues struggled financially and by 1976 the leagues proposed a merger. A class action lawsuit was filed by ABA players trying to prevent the merger. The eventual settlement included the NBA absorbing four ABA teams. The merger left the NBA with twenty-two teams, many in smaller markets. The National Basketball Association (NBA) did not match the numbers or the success of professional football or baseball during the 1970's. The television dollars didn't come close to those enjoyed by the other two major sports. ABC had the only rights to NBA games until 1973 when CBS bought those rights. In 1979 the NBA signed its first cable contract for a mere one and a half million dollars. 1970 was the first time that the NBA finals were televised in its entirety. By the late seventies the league was suffering from bad television ratings, financial issues, image problems and drug use. While the league suffered it continued to grow in number of teams. By the eighties there were twenty-three teams. I guess the leaders of the league felt like more teams in the league would translate into more fans and more interest. I'm not sure why they didn't realize that no matter how many teams you have, if ninety percent are still operating in the red, this is not progress. In the 1980's it came as no surprise to most that winning attracts fans. In 1984 the Chicago Bulls averaged less than six thousand actual fans in attendance. With the addition of Michael Jordan and a new winning attitude the Bulls tripled their attendance three years later. The Detroit Pistons were another prime example of what winning does. In 1980 they averaged five thousand fans per game. While winning the title in 1989 they averaged over twenty thousand fans per game. Television viewing was a different matter altogether. Television ratings were so bad in the decade that it became known as the "tape delayed" era. Games including playoffs would be taped and replayed at eleven thirty at night. In 1981 four games of the six NBA Finals were shown tape delayed. By 1986 all games were shown live thanks to the Larry Bird and Magic Johnson era. In 1984 the finals featuring these two stars drew the largest television audience in NBA history. By the 1990s the ratings started to once again decline. While Michael Jordan played the ratings remained stable but once he retired for good, the leagues savior was gone and so were many fans. From 2007-2019 ratings fell short of previous decades but were not the worst numbers in the history of the league. The same goes for actual game attendance. In 2007 overall attendance was over twenty two million, but by 2012 attendance dropped by over five million fans. The league never truly recovered after that fall in attendance and ratings.

If owners, management, and the players thought things couldn't get much worse, usher in 2020 the year of the Covid-19 virus or Covid-19 gimmick based on who you're talking to. Not only was 2020 the year of Covid-19, it was a year of riots, race related murders, and the Black Lives Matter movement. Covid-19 caused the NBA season to be shortened. The last portion of the season was played at Walt Disney World in Orlando Florida. All contending teams played the remainder of the regular season and the playoffs in the same arena with no fans allowed. The 2020 season which would normally wrap up in June was extended into October. The 2020-21 season that would have started in October 2020 was shortened and pushed to start in January 2021. Covid-19 was a big problem but fans reactions to the players during the period was even bigger. With the games just getting started back and the playoffs beginning all the teams refused to play games after a black man was shot by police in Wisconsin. If the NBA thought the fans reaction to the postponements was unsettling it was nothing compared to the reaction when players and entire teams knelt during the playing of the National Anthem. It was apparent the league had not learned from the plight of the National Football League. While all of these occurrences had an effect, the biggest effect was to the owner's pockets. Players still got paid, coaches still got paid, and rent was still being paid to the home facilities. All the while there were refunds for season tickets that were not honored. There was no parking revenue. There were no tickets sold. There were no concessions sold. There was no memorabilia being sold at the games. So, while the overhead of each team remained the same there was no funds being generated. It also didn't help matters that Lebron James the spokesman of the league started bombarding Americans and the media with his political beliefs when in reality nobody cared about his opinion. A Fox Network news host even went as far as to tell James to "shut up and dribble" If only LeBron James and the entire league had listened. The fans that the league lost due to the pandemic and the protest and the dollars lost by the league and its owners would eventually become the straw that broke the camel's back.

The NBA continued to lose fans in droves from 2020-2024. The millennials had no interest in professional basketball and then the millennial's kids spent more time on reality games than watching sports. The game had become boring even to hard core fans. From 2012-2025 the league became a predictable product with "super teams" winning every season from 2015-2024. First it was the Miami Heat with Lebron James, Dewayne Wade and company. That was followed by Stephen Curry, Kevin Durant, and an abundance of other all-stars leading the Golden State Warriors to consecutive titles losing only three playoff games in four years despite teams trying to catch up to them. When a reporter from the New York Times, prior to the season, correctly picked the NBA Champion and runner-up for seven straight years the league became "boring" for everyone. This boredom led to sell outs for the top three teams in the league but nearly empty arenas in the other twenty nine cities. Like the NFL, the answer to keeping the league in existence was to eliminate a number of teams that were costing the league money. In

2025 the NBA Board of Governors, NBA Commissioner Mr. Jordan, NBA Players Association, and the owners met in hopes of developing a long-term survival plan. Following the meeting a national news conference was held in downtown Chicago directed by Mr. Jordan. Mr. Jordan addressed those in attendance It is with great regret that I am here to inform you that the National Basketball Association is folding. A new league will be forming with twelve teams in twelve existing NBA cities. We have shut down all forms of minor league basketball. All existing players and coaches' contracts will be considered null and voided. All new contracts will be negotiated by the new teams after our initial draft. We intend to decrease the average player contract by over five thousand percent from NBA standards. Thus, the New American Basketball Association was formed. The NABA started play with twelve teams in the fall of 2026. The New York Knicks, Los Angeles Lakers, Chicago Bulls, Philadelphia 76er's, Boston Celtics, Dallas Mavericks, Miami Heat, Houston Rockets, Washington Wizards, Golden State Warriors, Cleveland Cavaliers, and Denver Nuggets would now make up the new NABA. The players from the dissolved teams had no problem finding work playing professional basketball overseas. The problem for the NBA was that these players were making more money overseas than the NBA teams could afford to pay its remaining players. Many of the star players joined their counterparts overseas not only for the increase in contracts but because the fan base was larger and the sport now more popular. One thing that the NABA failed to take in consideration was that by folding the NBA it not only cancelled players contracts but also the revenue from the previously signed television and sponsorship agreements. This oversight by the league cost the league billions of dollars in revenue. The previous television agreement guaranteed the NBA at least one televised game every day and all playoff games. The new contract guaranteed only a Saturday or Sunday game during the regular season and playoff games would be televised. The loss of this income prevented the owners from signing the star players. It also prevented upgrades in the arenas. The NABA would only last for one season. In

March 2026 Mr. Jordan held his final news conference. "Once again" he started. "I am here today with a very heavy heart. Professional basketball in America has come to an end. We have done everything we can do to save the league and to be honest, the fan base is just no longer strong enough to support the league. The leagues television viewership and game attendance has been on a roller coaster ride for over 70 years. In 1959 the league was struggling to survive with only 8 teams in operation. I really can't say exactly what happened to cause this demise. Some will say it was 2020 and the Covid-19 struggles. Others say it was the loss of fans during the protests of 2020. There are others including Business Insider that say it's because the NBA players were eighty percent black, ten percent foreign, and only ten percent white. Still others believe that the current generation just doesn't have very much interest in professional sports. Maybe everyone realized during the Corona-19 Pandemic that there were other things to occupy their time rather than watching or attendings sporting events. I'm not really sure what happened but please know that we gave every effort to continue professional basketball in America and all I can say is we failed. Thank you to all the owners, players, coaches and fans that have contributed over the past eighty years. I now invite you to ask any questions you may have because this will be the last news conference that we will hold." " Front row Bill? Jordan pointed toward reporter Bill Wise of the Chicago media. Mr. Jordan was asked if there was a chance the league or one like it was a possibility in the future? Mr. Jordan answered. "Well you can't ever say it will never happen but don't hold your breath. This group that is folding today was the best group of business men that we could assemble and they were not able to succeed. I don't know what anybody else could do different to succeed. It's not something I am interested in being involved in. Next question? " Will the league assist current coaches and players in finding new teams overseas or otherwise? "No" Jordan answered. "The league has folded...period. There will be no employees so therefore nobody will be employed to help the players and coaches. Those office people that lost their jobs today will be spending their time trying to find a job themselves. The players and coaches have agents to assist them so they'll be taken care of. Sports Channel host Ken Woos asked "When everything was revamped last year the plan sounded fool proof. So, what failed leading to today's decision"? The bottom line is as I said before. A lack of interest led to a lack of ticket sales, lack of concession sales, and lack of memorabilia sales. The old NBA team memorabilia sold five times more over the past year than the new league sold". The reason for the lack of interest is pretty obvious. First and foremost, there was no star power. Eighty of the top one hundred former NBA players signed contracts to play overseas where the game is becoming one of the most popular sports in the world. Professional basketball in America saw its most success when there were super star players like Larry Bird, Magic Johnson, myself, Lebron James and super teams like the old Lakers, Celtics, and Bulls. I think we were unable to provide anything like that for our fans. That is really all I can tell you. This will end the press conference. "Mr. Jordan, Mr. Jordan, Mr. Jordan we have more questions" the media yelled. Jordon turned and walked off of the stage as professional basketball in America ended.

O'Leary closed The Demise and remembered the day of that news conference. Professional basketball was never his favorite sport but he still hated seeing another sport die. He remembered thinking at the time that the changes made a year earlier would not save the league and then the mass exodus of the NBA's best players was the last nail in the coffin. O'Leary needed to get started on his upcoming owners meeting. As he was walking toward the elevator he started wondering if his new league would face the same fate that the new NBA had. After all the owners were all exceptional business men. They all thought they had put together a successful plan. The only difference he thought was that baseball was the oldest and lasted the longest. If nothing else it was America's game he thought. O'Leary got in and closed the door of his black Hummer. People asked why a billionaire drove a Hummer and not a Tesla? The answer was always the same. If he was involved in an accident he had a better chance of walking away uninjured. He drove to his home in anticipation of reading Rocket Beal's next article. He knew now that the articles would not assist him in his new venture but he loved Beal's uncensored honesty and his knowledge of the history of sports. He sat down in his favorite chair, opened his laptop and started reading the article.

# Chapter XIV

The only way to describe the decade of the eighties in sports or life in general in America was change, change, change. There are few decades that can compete with this decade as far as advancement of technology or the changes in attitudes and past traditions, not only in America but throughout the world. If you don't believe this you only have to look as far as the Berlin Wall constructed in 1961 to separate East and West Berlin, Germany. In 1989 the wall became nonexistent. Besides the changes of tradition in other countries the United States also saw traditions change. Route Sixty Six which was over two thousand miles long and created in the mid- sixties was removed from the list of highways in America. Route Sixty Six had once been the topic of movies, folklore, and even a television show named after it. Aside from the breaking of tradition there were many first during the 1980's. The video game Pac Man was invented, so was the Rubik's cube, Nintendo, the first mobile phone, and the first original Apple personal computer. The Oprah Winfrey show debut along with CNN, Raiders of the Lost Ark, and a little alien named ET. On the downside Americans were first introduced to a new drug called Crack which by 2020 had killed millions of people and destroyed many other lives. Another sad event of the 1980's was the assassination of one of the Beatles and one of the greatest song writers of all time John Lennon who was gunned down in front of his apartment in New York. The entire event and announcement of his death was played out nationwide by announcer Howard Cosell on the Monday Night Football telecast. Before I get into the sports history of the decade I must say that in my opinion the "great strides" we made were anything but that. PacMan,Nintendo, and the first mobile phones were anything but good in my opinion. So now instead of kids going outside and playing they sat inside on their ass and played video games. Instead of helping their parents with gardens or yard work they sat inside playing on their I Phone 800 or whatever number it was. Need proof? The rate of child and adolescent obesity more than tripled from the previous decade. Apple PC's and mobile phones caused way more problems than they solved. I don't even have to go into the statistics for you to realize how many crimes, accidents, deaths, murders, rapes, divorces, and the list goes on and on would have never happened without this advanced technology. OK now to sports in the decade. As with life in general there were many advancements in sports, many great teams, the introduction of many great players, along with scandals the sports world had never experienced before. While there were many great sports stories in the decade none could compare to the "Miracle on Ice". The United States Olympic hockey team made up of amateur players from the United States defeated a Russian Professional All-Star team four to three to win the Olympic Gold Medal. This still stands as the single greatest upset in all of Olympic history and maybe all of sports history. Just looking at a list of "newbies" in the 1980's lends anyone to believe that this decade was special. Michael Jordan, Joe Montana, Mike Tyson, Larry Bird, Magic Johnson, Bo Jackson, and the list goes on and on. Joe Montana gets my vote as GOAT (Greatest of all time) for NFL after leading the 49'ers to four Super Bowl titles, three of them in the eighties. Michael Jordan gets my vote as GOAT for the NBA and he entered his rookie campaign in 1984. Speaking of newbies, the decade started off with a bang. In baseball the 1980 World Series was a matchup of two teams with zero World Series titles combined. The Philadelphia Phillies defeated the Kansas City Royals to win its first world championship. There were two other baseball first in the decade. Jim Abbott ( California Angels) became the first one armed pitcher in the history of major league baseball. Abbott never spent a single day in the minor leagues and finished with 12 wins and 12 losses in his first season. Abbott would go on to win 87 games over 10 seasons including a no hitter in 1993. Another "first" occurred in 1986 when a World Series game was played indoors for the first time. The game was played inside the Metro dome in Minnesota between the home Twins and the visiting St. Louis Cardinals. The visiting Cardinals were unable to adjust to the indoors as they lost to the Twins four games to three, losing all four indoor games and winning all three games played outdoors. The following season the Chicago Cubs played the first ever night game at Wrigley Field in Chicago. The decade of first in baseball was also witness to Nolan Ryan pitching his fifth no hitter and Roger Clemons striking out twenty batters in one game. While the NFL and NBA was dominated by several teams Major League Baseball had nine champions in ten years with only the Los Angeles Dodgers winning twice. While there was unrest between players and owners throughout the decade the worst news of the decade came in 1989 when all times hit leader Pete Rose was banned from baseball for life for gambling on games. Let me make it very clear that Rose never bet against himself or his team. Over the years I've had a strong opinion that Rose should be allowed in the Hall of Fame. Many members of the Hall have done way worse.

The Olympics of the 1980's brought about many special moments including that USA Hockey upset. In 1984 Carl Lewis sprinted his way to four Gold medals at the Olympic games held in Los Angeles. He would eventually win nine Olympic Gold Medals in his career. The opposite side of the coin occurred four years later in the 1988 games in Seoul South Korea when USA sprinter Ben Johnson was stripped of his hundred meter Gold Medal after testing positive for a banned substance. I witnessed the race as it happened and I still believe that performance was one of the best I have ever seen. If not for the failed test it would still be considered an unmatched feat.

The NBA rebounded during the 1980's. At the end of the 1970's the NBA fan base and television ratings were declining at a rapid pace. The league adopted the three point shot. The new rule may have helped but it was the players and the teams that increased the fan base and the television viewership. Early in the decade in 1980 a rookie Ervin Magic Johnson took the league by storm along with fellow rookie Larry Bird. In the NBA finals the Lakers were matched up against the Philadelphia 76er's. In game five of the series league most valuable player Kareem Abdul Jabbar was injured. Jabbar was a seven-foot center. The next game Magic Johnson moved from his normal point guard position normally the shortest player on the court, and replaced Jabbar at center. Most thought this would never work. That night in his only game at the center position Johnson finished with 42 points and 15 rebounds leading the Lakers to the title. Over the next nine years the Magic Johnson and Larry Bird duels led to five championships for the Johnson led Lakers and three titles for Bird and his Boston Celtics during the decade. This decade was one of the most successful in the history of the sport.

The NFL continued to strive during this decade. Television ratings were up. The number of games televised increased. The sport continued to provide great players, great games, and great teams. The team of the decade is not considered the best team of the decade. The Joe Montana led San Francisco 49ers was the team of the decade winning three Super Bowls and adding a forth in 1990. While this run was impressive, it paled when comparing any of those teams with the 1985 Chicago Bears. The Bears were led by a lot of special characters including Walter "sweetness" Payton, wild and crazy quarterback Jim McMann, and nearly four hundred pound William "Refrigerator" Perry. Perry was a defensive tackle that was used as a running back when the Bears were close to the goal line. The team finished the season with fifteen wins and only one loss. They won their two playoff games by a combined score of forty five to nothing. They followed those wins with a forty six to ten trouncing of the New England Patriots in Super Bowl twenty. Free agency led players to leave the Bears prior to the next season. They still finished with only two losses in 1986 but lost in the first round of the playoffs. The 1980's were dominated by three teams the 49ers won three titles, the Washington Redskins won two and the Oakland Raiders won two. Those three teams combined for seven of the ten Super Bowl winners.

Major college sports continued to thrive. College football was attracting some of the largest crowds in history. The National Champion was still being voted on in the eighties which led to many disputes about who really was the best team in the nation. Because conference champions were locked into certain bowl games it was rare for the two best teams to ever meet to determine the champion. During the decade the Miami Hurricanes won three national titles. No other team won more than one. On a darker side of college football, the Southern Methodist University football team became the first team in history to receive the "death penalty" from the NCAA. The penalty prevented the Mustangs from fielding a team in 1987 and they could play no home games in 1988. The school itself imposed an additional ban as it was unable to field a competitive team. The penalty would prove deadly as SMU would have only one winning season over the next twenty years. That would become the first and to date, the last death penalty given out by the NCAA at any level.

The 1980's would provide some of the best and most exciting college basketball history including what was considered at the time to be the biggest upset in NCAA tournament history. In 1983 the N.C. State Wolfpack entered the NCAA tournament as a sixth seed and twenty-fourth seed overall. They had to win the Atlantic Coast Conference tournament to even qualify for the NCAA tournament because they finished in 4th place in the conference with an eight win and six loss record. In round one of the ACC tournament they won by one point over Wake Forest. In the next round they upset defending National Champion UNC in overtime. In the ACC finals they upset second seed Virginia by three. The Pack won three games by a total of nine points. NCSU opened the NCAA tournament with a two-point victory over Pepperdine. That was followed by a one point victory over UNLV. They then trounced a favored Utah team. In the west Region finals, the Pack once again upset top seed Virginia by one point. In the final four they defeated Georgia to advance to the title game where they would face a University of Houston team led by five future NBA players. The NC

State squad entered the game as a seven point underdog. They ended the game with a two point victory on a last second put back dunk. That play and the video of Coach Jim Valvano running around the court looking for somebody to hug would be a staple highlight of the NCAA tournament until its end. The decade produced nine different NCAA Champions and March Madness was becoming one of the most anticipated sporting events in all of sports.

The 1980's also produced many exciting moments for what most consider minor sports. Greg Lemond became the first American to win the Tour De France in 1986. Mike Tyson and Sugar Ray Leonard dominated the boxing world. During the decade Tyson won thirty seven straight bouts, thirty three of them by knockout and seventeen of them were won in the first round. Leonard won ten of eleven fights with his only loss being to Roberto Duran known as "Hand of Stone". The highlight in the world of golf was the 1986 Masters championship won by Jack Nickolas at forty six years of age.

Soccer continued to gain in popularity worldwide and the BBC televised its first soccer game in 1983. The BBC now televises hundreds of games every year. In the United States the supporters of the sport hoped to capitalize on the popularity of the North American Soccer League. They targeted the 1984 Olympics and the 1986 World Cup as a means to create interest in the sport while rebuilding its national team. From 1980-1983 the national team had only competed twice in International matches. The US team had a decent Olympics finishing with a one win, one loss, and one draw record. They did not advance past the first stage. By 1984 the NASL had folded decreasing the once growing popularity of the sport in America. Qualifying for the World Cup would have created great interest in America. In order to qualify for the World Cup, the US National team would only need to win a home game against a Costa Rica squad they'd defeated handily earlier in the year. For some reason the game was played in Torrance California an area populated mostly by Costa Rica residents. The game was marketed primarily to the Costa Rican community even providing Costa Rican dancers for the halftime entertainment. Costa Rica all of a sudden was the home team and pulled out the upset eliminating the US team from World Cup competition. I wondered then and still wonder forty four years later how and who was able to pull this off. This once again set the sport back while it excelled all over the world.

The best word to describe the decade known as the 1980's a decade of "first". The decade provided many great teams, players, games, and probably the most successful financially decade is the history of sports. By the next decade things were changing all over the world and all over the world of sports. Fans had no idea what the future would bring over the next ten years".

O'Leary finished reading the article and his first thought was how much had occurred in the world of sports in the past thirty years and then all of a sudden, it's gone. While he certainly understood the financial struggles involved in professional sports, he still didn't fully understand the collapse.

# Chapter XV

The following morning O'Leary finished his breakfast and went for his usual morning run. As he passed by the park he noticed how many people utilized the park. There were parents with young children, teenagers, older couples, people walking dogs or dogs walking people in some cases. He spotted an old man and woman enjoying the sunshine and feeding the birds and squirrels. He thought he recognized him and the closer he got he realized it was Rocket Beal himself. He had never met Beal but had always wanted to. He went up to Beal and introduced himself apologizing for bothering him but Beal was happy to meet him. O'Leary went on and on about how much he was enjoying the articles and how much he's enjoyed listening to Beal's broadcast over the years. Before they knew it over an hour had passed. Manna took Floyd Beal by the arm and told him it was time to go. It'd taken her an hour to convince Beal to go with her into the city for a doctor's appointment, then another hour coaxing him into having lunch at the park. Now he was ready to stay and chat about sports for hours. It was a thirty mile drive back into the country side to Beal's modest home. Before Beal and Manna could leave O'Leary took the moment to run his new idea by the old announcer. If he knew one thing about Beal it was he'd get an honest no holds barred opinion. After hearing all of the details Beal was highly impressed with the ideas. He told O'Leary that his ideas were "old school" ideas. He thought the shortened season, less travel, lower overhead, lower salaries, and weekend only games were all good ideas. "I'll tell you what Mr. O'Leary." Beal said "I'm going to use a portion of an article to promote your idea. I believe that most sports fans would jump at the chance to watch professional baseball again. " O'

Leary left the chance meeting feeling great after getting Rocket Beal's approval and an endorsement in his article would go a long way in convincing fans to want a piece of his new league. O' Leary's dream team worked hard the following week preparing for the owners' meetings and follow-up press conference. The initial owners meeting was held at the old Sears Tower in Chicago. As O' Leary entered the room he was greeted by an unexpected ovation from the potential owners, network execs, and special friends. He couldn't believe how great everything looked. O'Leary left the decorations and the food and drink to Paul and Sarah McGovern. They had an enormous amount of experience in social gatherings and they came through once again. The decor consisted of red, white and blue drapery around the top of the entire room. Behind the podium was a twenty-foot American flag and another flag with the new league American Baseball League ABL logo. Each owner had his own table dressed out in shooting star table clothes and a large baseball center piece. O'Leary was impressed and hoped everyone else would be. If they didn't care for the decorations they'd love the food and drink table. How could you not like the most famous recipes from each participating city prepared by a Top Chef winning chef. As everyone mingled O'Leary sat with his wife, the McGovern's, and Frank and Mike Riley, all major members of O'Leary's dream team. O'Leary stepped to the podium and received a very unexpected standing ovation. That was a good sign he thought, now if he could just get the fans to have that same enthusiasm. "Good Morning to all. A very special welcome to our twelve owners. We are happy to have all of you on this exciting day. Our team will outline the details of the league. The media will later be provided with the same details we are providing you today. One by one O'Leary, McGovern, and the Riley's all presented the outlines for the league.

O'Leary ended the meeting by telling all of those in attendance "There are forms on each table explaining how to present questions or ideas to the league office. We thank you for your time today and we look forward to working together to make the new league successful and bring back the excitement of professional baseball to where it belongs, in America!"

As O'Leary left the room he was greeted by a hoard of television cameras, microphones, reporters, and photographers. O'Leary had to admit he was shocked at the interest the league was already generating. There wasn't this much coverage when the league had folded. "Ladies and Gentleman you will be provided with the minutes of our meeting later today via email. I will confirm that there are plans in the works for a new professional baseball league in America. The email you will receive shortly will answer most if not all of your questions.

The more O'Leary analyzed his plan in his mind the more convinced he was there was great reason for his optimism. His plans will guarantee that owners make a profit, stadiums make a profit, and there will be no way for anyone to lose money, unless of course teams couldn't attract even three thousand fans. The thought almost made him sick. Another positive detail was some players may still be able to make more than a million dollars a year in salary and playoff winnings. That should be enough to attract some very good talent to the league. He told himself that there will never be a contract paying a guaranteed sixty thousand dollars per every at bat like Alex Rodriquez enjoyed. That is what destroyed professional baseball to begin with. If Rodriquez went to bat five times in a game it cost his team almost three hundred thousand dollars in one night. How many fifteen dollar beers, twelve dollar hot dogs and three hundred dollar tickets would the team have to sell just to pay for that one night's five at bats? Now we'll have five dollar hot dogs, five dollar beers, affordable tickets, free parking and everyone will profit, including the owners, players and yes, the fans.

Floyd Beal called Joe Mills as soon as he saw the news was breaking. He already mentioned his park encounter with O'Leary to Mills but Mills wasn't so sure the dream would become a reality. When Floyd told Mills the who's who of the owners that attended the meeting, all he had to say was "Well those owners have enough wealth to withstand any losses if the league fails." I'm really looking forward to going to a game. Beal responded "Me too, I hope I live long enough to see opening day". Beal couldn't spend any more time on the rotary phone, he had an article to write. Manna walked into the room surprised at how spry and happy he seemed. "Well I haven't seen you this happy in a while" "Well I'm going to a baseball game; never thought I'd get to do that again". She just looked at him thinking he might live to see it, but would he even know what he was watching or would he even be alive? She'd seen him go downhill quick since the diagnosis. "Where's my Shine?" he asked. Well he hasn't forgot about that stuff she thought to herself. Two weeks later Beal's fifth article was published. Manna would soon realize she was going to help a lot more with this article. Beal would start speaking into his micro pen and would start talking about his wife or a vacation they took. Then when she'd remind him of what he was supposed to be doing, he'd snap out of it and get back on task, with her help. She'd helped him throughout but as Floyd Beal's memory deteriorated he'd been asked to write the articles bi-weekly instead of monthly. If only they knew how hard this was for both of them. The day before the deadline the micro penned article was finished and transferred via "space" as Beal would say to the New York Times newspaper for publication. She read it to Beal the next day. This time he didn't complain about her wanting to read to him. She knew this wasn't a good sign.

# Chapter XVI

M anna started reading: By the time the 1990's rolled out its carpet, the world and the United States was becoming a totally different place to live. It was a world that would further separate generations and families and lead to far more destruction than good. Innovative inventions that could have had a positive impact on the world were used instead to destroy and corrupt people, places, and eliminate many of the valuable traditions older generations had worked hard to create and maintain. Not only did the electronics revolution advance computers, websites, and gaming systems, it also led to more advanced mechanics used to create havoc in bombings and terrorism. In 1993 a truck bomb exploded at the World Trade Center killing 6 people and injuring over 1000 more. Two years later a bomber struck in Oklahoma City killing 168 people. Bombings even effected the world of sports. A year after the Oklahoma City bombing a bomb was detonated at City Center at the Olympics being held in Atlanta. The bomb killed one and injured over a hundred others. By the mid 1990's people were starting to fear bombers and random violence so going out in public became risky to many. It seemed to me looking back at the times that people in general quit caring about others and day to day life became much more dangerous than in previous decades. Kids couldn't even go to school without risk. In 1999 two students walked into Columbine High school and assassinated thirteen fellow students starting a sad trend that would continue for decades to come. The only risk my generation faced at school was getting hurt in gym class. For those of you that don't know what gym class is, they changed the name to physical education. Changing the name must have decreased participation because there were more obese children than ever before in the 1990's. Oh there was a reason the 1990's continued to increase obesity in America . Kids didn't just have to sit on their ass and play video games at home, because by 1995 they were introduced to the Gameboy that allowed them to sit on their ass and play video games anywhere and everywhere they went. Everywhere I went there were kids consumed or a better word may be possessed by the video games. I never understood the video game obsession. I just think that mind games like chess, checkers, and scrabble were much more beneficial mentally. While I'm on toys of the 90's can someone tell me what the hell is a furry and what's its purpose? I also thought that baseball, basketball, football, or even horse shoes was much more beneficial physically than setting on one's ass exercising their fingers. I think I read somewhere that moving fingers burns six calories per hour. Look it up. Video games were just a small portion of computerization advancement. Just in this decade alone, the world wide web was launched in 1991, Apple revealed its first iMac which would become known as the best computer in existence. The bidding on anything web site eBay was founded in 1995. Three years later the search engine Google went online and became the most popular search engine in history. While the United States appeared to be going to hell in a hand basket there were some great things going on in other parts of the world. The communist USSR was dissolved and the country became known as Russia. Nelson Mandala was released in 1990 after being held captive for many years. Four years later he would be elected as President of South Africa. The Hobble telescope made space a place that could be viewed continuously. Sports in America would be no different than what was going everywhere else. Need proof? There was murder! Football great O.J. Simpson was found not guilty of a double homicide that clearly divided races and caused racial tension in America. All evidence pointed directly toward a guilty verdict but a jury of twelve peers ruled otherwise. There was drug use! By 1991 a major league baseball player, an NBA player and an NFL player were all banned for life for drug use. Hall of Fame football player Lyle Alzado blamed his brain tumor on steroid use. There was greed! In 1991 alone MLB player Bobby Bonilla signed a twenty nine million-dollar contract, NBA player Patrick Ewing signed a thirty three-million-dollar contract, and NFL QB Dan Marino signed a twenty five-million-dollar contract. There was rape! Boxer Mike Tyson not only lost his title early in the decade, he also lost his freedom when he was given a six-year prison sentence after being found guilty of rape. There was assault! During training for the 1994 Olympics figure skater Nancy Kerrigan was attacked by two men allowing underdog Tanya Harding to prevail. Days later, Harding's boyfriend and an accomplish were arrested for the attack. Harding would eventually be charged with conspiracy. There was kidnapping! Boxer Riddick Bowe was charged and convicted of kidnapping his estranged wife and five children. There was Aids. Magic Johnson retired from the game after being HIV positive. I could go on and on but I know you want to read something positive. I'm showing you the negatives of the decade in sports so you can better understand how much things changed. There had never been a decade where sports figures went from being respected hero's to disrespected villains and criminals.

During the 1990's despite the negative issues and publicity, most sports continued to thrive including soccer which would take the nation by surprise. While all sports remained steady, one stood out above all. Nascar racing would have its best decade in the history of the sport. The "King of Nascar" Richard Petty would end his illustrious career in 1992 that included more than two hundred checkered flags.. While Petty was leaving the sport there were many drivers that were prepared to step up and take his place. A young driver by the name of Jeff Gordan would make his debut. By 1995 this young charismatic driver would win his first Nascar title. He would eventually be inducted into the Nascar Hall of Fame. Both attendance and viewership would continue to grow by leaps and bounds. Another fan favorite was veteran Dale Earnhardt better known as "The Intimidator" for his aggressive no apologies style of driving. The sport was becoming so popular even Hollywood got involved with the filming of Days of Thunder. In 1990 there were twenty nine races at twelve different speedways. By 1999, there were thirty-seven races at twenty different tracks. The expansion would introduce Nascar racing to new fans all over the country with races in the north, south, east and west regions of the country. Nascar would soon come to learn that maybe they should have added races but not tracks. This is the last I'll say about Nascar in my articles because the stupidity of what destroyed this "sport" is too much for an old man like me to comprehend or understand, much less convey to you.

The 1990's would also prove to be some of the best and most lucrative years in the history of the NBA. Riding the coattails of the 80's with the Larry Bird (Celtics) and Magic Johnson (Lakers) feuds, the NBA was about to be introduced to the next savior of the league...Michael Jordan. The NBA in the 90's was dominated by the Chicago Bulls and was led by still the greatest of all time Michael Jordan. The Bulls won six titles during the 1990's. They did this by keeping the team together during the title runs unlike the so-called super teams and superstars of the following decades. Adding to the excitement of the Bulls was the fact that there were other great teams during the decade that in any other era could have won multiple titles. When Michael Jordan retired for two years to pursue a baseball career in 1994, the Houston Rockets capitalized on Jordan's absence by winning back to back titles. Upon Jordan's return the Bulls would continue to dominate the league. I have to mention another great team that was denied a title during the decade. The Utah Jazz led by hall of famers Karl Malone and John Stockton were knocked out of finals by the Jordan led Bulls in 1998 and 1999. I have always considered this the best team to never win a title. With the NBA interest skyrocketing in the late 1980's television would prove to be huge! CBS carried all NBA games for seventeen years. In the final four years from 1986-1990 CBS paid nearly fifty million dollars per season. In 1989 NBC paid over three times that amount for the telecast rights through 1994. It didn't take long for the rights to pay off big for the new network. NBA viewers increased to an all-time high. When Jordan returned in 1995 from his baseball journey his first game back was the most watched regular season game in NBA history. In 1998 the NBA finals attracted the most viewers in history. By the following season which was marred by a labor lockout the number of viewers plummeted to the lowest numbers of the decade. Little did the NBA know the trend would continue. While television viewers increased significantly during the decade attendance figures stayed flat. In 1990 the average NBA attendance was less than sixteen thousand per game. By 1999 the average was the same.

While the NBA was searching for success, the NFL was excelling beyond belief. The teams, the players, the new stadiums and the competition continued to impress fans leading to an increase in attendance and television viewers. Nearly every decade had a team of the decade and this decade was no different. The team of the nineties was the Dallas Cowboys. They became the first team in history to win three Super Bowls in four seasons. While the Cowboys were the big winners, the big losers of the decade were the Buffalo Bills. As an old man I still feel sorry for Bills fans. Not really. Buffalo lost four consecutive Super Bowls. The player list from the decade is like a who's who of NFL history. Dan Marino became the all-time leading passer; San Francisco wide receiver Jerry Rice became the all-time leader in reception yards and all-time touchdown leader. Detroit Lions great Barry Sanders rushed for over two thousand yards. The league introduced fifteen new or renovated stadiums to its fans. All of this led to an increase in attendance every year of the decade. The 1993 Super Bowl drew almost a hundred thousand fans which was the most in league history and still stood as the second highest attended Super Bowl when the league folded.

The 1990's for Major League Baseball was a decade of the historical records, historical players, historical games, and historical revenue. The problem with the game was that the historical revenue and historical greed caused historically stupid decisions. The player strike of 1994-95 cost teams games during both seasons including the 1994 post season playoffs. It would be the first time in ninety years that there was no World Series. This strike was seen as the lowest point in baseball history even topping the Black Sox scandal of 1909. Fans were angry going as far as burning tickets, memorabilia, and swearing to never watch another game. Nobody realized it at the time but many of the former fans started following the sport of soccer, but more on that later. While fans blamed the players, the owners were as much if not more at fault. Unlike other sports, the owners played "we take all". On the field the New York Yankees used the large market money to win three World Series in the decade. The team of the decade was the same as the choker of the decade. Despite making the playoffs every season of the decade, and going to five World Series, the Atlanta Braves came away with only one title. So yes, Braves fans, this old man feels sorry for you too. Not really! As for the players and the game itself, the word of the decade was "juiced". Juiced baseballs and juiced players were the topic of the decade. Thirteen of the top fifty home run seasons in history was recorded during the decade including four of the top six. Fans used common sense and realized that something was rotten not only in in St. Louis, but in Chicago, San Francisco, and cities across the country. The fans and media started accusing the league of juicing the baseball to regain fans interest. They also accused the players of taking steroids which the players denied, well for a while. How else could they explain topping Babe Ruth's sixty homer run season four times over two seasons. Attendance pre-strike was at an all-time high. In 1991,92,and 93 the four million attendance mark was surpassed four times. This was the first time in history this mark had been reached by any team. Nine teams set all time attendance records but six of those were achieved pre-strike. From pre-strike to post strike the average team attendance dropped by thirty three percent. Attendance would never fully recover during the decade. By the end of the decade attendance was still down by over ten percent.

Soccer continued to increase in popularity in America. In 1990 the U.S. national team competed in the World Cup for the first time in forty years. The World Soccer League and the American Soccer League merged to form the American Professional Soccer League. The following year the US Women's team captured the first ever FIFA World championship. They would also capture the Pan Am games. As with any other sport, success breeds interest and sports fans across America started taking notice. In 1993 the first strategic session was held in Chicago. At this meeting two hundred and fifty soccer players, coaches, and officials met to develop a plan for soccer entering the twenty first century. In 1994 the greatest worldwide sporting event the World Cup was held in America. I covered many of the games and while I've never been a huge fan of the sport, I must say it was one of the most exciting sporting events I ever had the opportunity to cover. I wasn't the only one that felt that way. More than three million fans attended the World Cup event breaking the overall attendance record by more than a million fans. Both men and women national teams continued to shock the soccer world with their continued success. The women's team captured the Gold medal at the 1994 Olympics. While the men's team faltered in the 1998 World Cup the US Women won the 1999 Women's World Cup in front of ninety thousand fans at the Rose Bowl in Pasadena California. This victory set off a soccer hysteria in America. The victorious women appeared on the cover of Time, Newsweek, People and Sports Illustrated magazines. They also enjoyed a visit to the White House. Soccer in America was climbing to another level in the USA. Other sports were starting to lose its hero's and in turn lose its fans. Sports like boxing, tennis and golf all lost the names that'd made them so popular. No more Muhammad Ali, George Foreman, Ken Norton, no more Chrissy Evert, Billie Jean King, or Martina Navratilova, no more Jack Nickels, Lee Trevino, and the list went on. The best way to sum up sports in the decade is to say it was the decade where innocence was lost, greed outweighed common sense and negative reality was reigning supreme.

Joe Mills read the article and immediately realized that his friend Floyd was getting more and more cynical as time went by. He hoped it was just him being an old ornery man and not a result of the disease advancing. He couldn't blame his friend for his negative attitude.

Reading each article and how things were changing was like watching a plane fly slowly toward a brick wall. He scrolled down to the next page and saw an article about one of the new owners, New York Empires owner Burt Smith. Smith had a massive heart attack and was in intensive care. Smith and Mills had known each other for many years. They weren't really friends but had been to many of the same parties, fund raisers and other events. As he finished his thoughts his phone rang, Joe actually had a cell phone. He answered and it was O'Leary on the phone. O'Leary informed him that Mr. Smith had passed away. He knew that Smith's family would no longer wish to own the new team. O'Leary was sad to learn of his friend's death. They'd just had lunch a few days earlier. Smith had been so excited about owning a team and about professional baseball returning. Now he'd never get to see the outcome. While he was sad he knew he'd have to find a new owner as soon as possible. He went on with the conversation. He wanted to know if Mills and possibly Floyd Beal would like to purchase the franchise. He figured who better than a former writer and a former announcer to run a team? He knew between the two they could easily come up with the two-million-dollar price tag and both had a good business sense. He also knew that despite covering nearly every sport possible, both men professed to baseball being their favorite and the one they missed most. Mills was floored at the offer. He'd jump at the chance if Floyd was in better health but he wasn't sure he'd want to do this on his own. He'd also jump at the chance if he didn't have to tell Bea. She wouldn't be happy. She might not ever cook chicken pie again. He'd need time to think about it and also see if Floyd would even be interested. Joe was all smiles when he got off the phone. As Bea entered the room she said "Joe Mills, what are you up to? I haven't seen you smile like that since you proposed". Joe laughed at her said "Well dear I have another proposal for you? " She just shook her head. Somehow, she knew her promised time with Joe was going to be put on hold yet again. She would have never dreamed as to the reason why. All she knew was that her husband had been promising to retire for years so they could spend more time with the kids, grandkids and each other. It seemed to Bea that he'd been busy from the time they met in grade school up until now. Throughout grade school, high school and college Joe spent the majority of his time studying his subjects and studying sports. He took great pride in making straight A's all the way through school and being valedictorian of his high school class. They started dating after they reconnected at his surprise birthday party following his graduation from St. Johns. From then on it was work, work, work. He worked and she was what he called a professional home maker. He had provided a wonderful life for her and the family and she understood this took most of his time. Now what was he up to she thought? He walked into the kitchen and sat down with a beer. "You want a beer or a glass of wine or maybe a shot of Floyd's moonshine" ? He asked. "You're probably going to need it."

# Chapter XVII

The following morning Joe got ready and called Floyd. Manna answered the phone and told him that Joe was pretty drunk the night before and was still in bed. Joe told her that Floyd's recent excessive drinking was worrying him. She told him " well Joe, he's depressed about his illness and he's bored. He knows once he finishes the articles there's nothing else left but for him to die. He's bored, he has nothing to do with his time, nothing else to live for". Joe thought he had a surprise in store for her and his friend Floyd. There's plenty left for Floyd to get excited about, he thought, like owning a professional baseball team. He told her to get him out of bed and drive him to the city. They'd all meet at two sharp at their favorite restaurant Beefy Boys. To say Beefy Boys had a limited menu would be an over statement. They only served Big Uns, a two-pound monster burger, Lil Uns, a beef slider with grilled onions and A-1 sauce, and Chicago style hot dogs. House cut fries on the side and the best milk shakes in the city. That was the full menu but the food was worth waiting in the long lines for. Joe got to Beefy's an hour before he was to meet Floyd and Manna. He'd thought of every angle he could use to talk Floyd into joining him in ownership of the team. He had already decided he wouldn't buy the team on his own if Beal wasn't interested. Now it was an opportunity to give his friend something to do to keep him busy. He knew his odds of talking Floyd into it were very slim if not impossible. He could hear him now "Hell No Joe, are you crazy, I'm a ninety year old man with a mind debilitating disease. I don't have the energy or the desire to own a baseball team" end of conversation. Joe was seated just before two. He'd already been to the counter and ordered for himself, Floyd, and Manna. It was easy, they'd both ordered the same thing several hundred times before. Manna was easy to please so he just guessed she'd like two Lil Ones and a milk shake. the same as Beal. Joe always got the Big Un all the way with fries and a water. He and Floyd always laughed that he'd eat a two pound burger all the way but wouldn't get a shake because he was watching his weight. Floyd loved the Lil Un's because of the grilled onions and A-1 sauce and he always got a large chocolate milkshake with an extra scoop of ice cream. Just as the food arrived at the table Floyd and Manna arrived and he was happy he wouldn't have to stand in the even longer line now. "This better be good you got me out of bed while I was enjoying a massive hangover" he laughed. Joe didn't beat around the bush and just came right out and proposed the offer to Beal. " Floyd, Mr. O'Leary called me yesterday and asked if you and I would be interested in purchasing the New York Empires for two million dollars". Beal leaned over toward a dreaded Mills and said "Joe are you pulling my leg?" Joe shook his head no. He looked at Manna and asked her if he could afford it. She hesitated before telling him he indeed had enough money to buy in. "Hell, yea I winna own the Empires! They'll be amazing. Are you crazy? I'll be at every game cheering on our team. So, when do we start"? Joe was in shock. They made plans to meet at O'Leary's office to sign all of the papers and produce the payment to finalize the deal. When Joe got home he broke the news to Bea. He knew she wouldn't be happy. Sports wasn't really her thing and she was still left waiting on the time with Joe she'd been promised when he retired. While she wasn't thrilled she was supportive as always. She knew deep inside that if anybody could make this work, those two friends could. She was a little worried about Beal's health but Joe assured her they'd cross that bridge when they got to it. "So, you're not retiring and we're not traveling, right"? Yes, he was retiring from the paper as soon as possible so he could take on this new adventure. Mills made the call to O'Leary and he agreed to meet the following day to finalize the deal. Joe went into the newspaper office the next day and wrote his final article. It simply said " I just bought the New York Empires I'm outta here. Thanks for the memories. Joe thought that Mr. Wiseman would be upset but he was actually happy for Joe Mills. He realized Joe could have retired years ago. Beal and Manna went home and discussed exactly what an owner a team owner does. "I think they sat in the stands and drink beer and eat peanuts and cracker Jacks. She laughed out loud thinking he was really losing his mind fast. She was even more dumbfounded when he didn't ask for his shine later that night. She asked him if he wanted a drink and he told her that he had work to do. He wanted to get his articles finished so he could start working on his duties as owner, like watch baseball games. That night he completed the upcoming article without any help from Manna. Maybe this was just the medicine he needed. He'd written:

Well it's good to be back. I'm nearing the end of my eight-month assignment. This is number six. As I look back on my articles to date, I hate to say this but the world in general including the world of sports has not improved and is becoming a meaner, greedier, less feeling, less caring, more violent, political ball of hell waiting to explode. The biggest event of the decade was Y2K. The citizens of the United States prepared for the events of Y2K like it was a newly discovered creature. Y2K stands for the year two thousand. Many feared that by the calendar turning to the year two thousand, computers would be rendered useless. The fearful believed that anything controlled by computers including power plants, prison security, retail stores, air travel, and numerous other essentials would be shut down by the "Millennium Bug". The fear of course was unfounded and the new century began without a glitch. That was about the only thing going smooth. In 2001 the US invaded Afghanistan and toppled the evil Taliban. Twenty years later they gave it back. Also, in 2001 the largest terrorist attack in U.S.history occurred at the World Trade Center in New York. Two planes hijacked by terrorist were flown into the Twin Towers and the buildings collapsed killing nearly three thousand people. In 2003 the United States Military invaded Iraq. The invasion would last until 2009. More than four thousand American lives were lost. In 2007 America suffered its worst recession since the Great Depression. Computerization continued to terrorize America. The Facebook site was founded in 2004. I have always believed that sites like that are the work of the devil. This site caused too many crimes to even get into so we'll leave it at that. My question is What good did Facebook ever do? I'm sure someone from the infant generation will come up with some lame answer. The decade was one of ups and downs for the major sports in America. I stated in my previous article that I won't address Nascar anymore. If you want to know the inside scoop on what happened to those greedy bumbling idiots, just read my friend Joe Mills book, The Demise. I must however address two of the top Nascar stories of the decade. "The Intimidator" Dales Earnhardt was killed in a freak accident in Daytona, Florida. On a happier note a female, Danica Patrick became the first woman of the new racing area to be signed to a Nascar deal. About her, "The King" Richard Petty would eventually say "The only way she'll ever win a race is if she's the only one on the track". As a sports enthusiast I hoped that the negative things about sports in the 1990's would be a learning experience and things would improve in the new decade and new century. It didn't. During the decade one in every forty-five NFL players was arrested, so more than one on every team. The NBA percentages were nearly identical. NBA super star Kobe Bryant was charged with rape. The National Hockey League learned nothing from Major League Baseball and there was a lockout in 2004-05. NBA referee Tim Donaghy was charged with betting on games he officiated. Steroids ran rampant in every sport. Even track and field couldn't escape the decade unscathed as five-time Olympic medalist Marion Jones admitted to steroid use and was forced to give up the five medals she'd won. By 2004 baseball was testing for any performance enhancing drugs. There was bad news for sports in general as all three major sports in America had all-time lows in television viewership. The viewership was not the only thing to decline. The number of fans in attendance also continued to decrease.

Major League baseball spent the decade trying to recover from the strike the decade before. The league continued to hope that more excitement would increase interest, game attendance and television ratings. What could add more excitement than a home run barrage? Nobody comes to a game to see a 1-0 or 2-1 game. If they say they do, they are in the same boat as old Nascar fans that said they didn't go to races to see the wrecks. If you think I'm wrong, just watch fans reaction in baseball when a homer occurs and when a wreck occurs in Nascar. The fans were aware of wide spread steroid use thanks in part to a Sports Illustrated article in which former Most Valuable Player Ken Carminati stated that fifty percent of all MLB players used steroids. The fans and pitchers also believed in the juiced ball theory. The numbers would back up the theories. In 2000 there were over five thousand home runs hit. For the second consecutive year ten teams hit at least two hundred home runs. Hell, that's not hard to do when one player hits seventy, another hits sixty, and the list went on. In July 2002 there were sixty-two home runs hit in one day, the most in history. There were a lot of other first that didn't have anything to do with steroids or juiced baseballs. The 2001 World Series became the only one in history to end in November after the season was extended after the September terrorist attacks. In 2000 the Chicago Cubs defeated the New York Mets in a game held in Tokyo Japan. The game was the first major league game played outside of North America. In one of the worst decisions ever made that effected not just baseball but all sports was when the Texas Rangers signed Alex Rodriquez to a ten year two hundred fifty-two-million-dollar contract. There was so much wrong with this. Of course, this would lead to higher salary demands, higher ticket prices, higher concession prices, higher parking prices, need I say more?

While there was a lot going on off the field there was a lot happening on the field. The New York Yankees appeared in four World Series and won two of them. Their arch rival the Boston Red Sox also won two. The remaining six championships was split between six teams. As far as rebounding from the strike plagued decade before, the numbers were mixed causing opinions to differ as to whether the game was recovering its fan base. Attendance increased over the previous decade by about eighteen percent. While this looked good on paper, the numbers didn't take into consideration that many games were cancelled because of the strike. Realistically the average number of fans attending the games was about equal to the previous decade. The tell tell sign for me back then was looking at the World Series television numbers. Since I was announcing many of the games, I took great interest in how many people watched and listened. The World Series throughout history had been the most watched baseball games in history. People that weren't even fans would tune in to the games. At the beginning of the decade eighteen million fans tuned in to view the games. By 2010 there were only fourteen million viewing. This was the forty first lowest rating out of forty-six years of televised coverage. Compare this to the all-time best of forty-four million views in 1978. A decrease of nearly seventy percent. MLB's popularity continued to slide.

The NBA had just completed its two most successful decades in history. The NBA was going to have to try to keep the fans interest without the likes of the Magic Johnson's, Larry Bird's, and Michael Jordan's. The other issue was the lack of rivalries. There was no Lakers and Celtics of the eighties, no Bulls verses Pistons or Knicks in the nineties, it was a decade starting fresh looking to capitalize on the previous decade's popularity. The decade was dominated by the large market Los Angeles Lakers and small market San Antonio Spurs. The Lakers led by future hall of Famers Kobe Bryant and Shaquille O'Neal appeared in seven NBA finals winning five of them. The Spurs appeared in and won three titles. Some interesting notes from the decade included the fact that Michael Jordan returned to the game in 2001, not with the Bulls but with the Washington Wizards. You know they changed the name from Bullets to Wizards in 1997 because Bullets caused death. Well so do Lions, Tigers, and Bears, oh no, so does Gators and well you get the point. In an amazing performance Kobe Bryant scored 81 points against the New York Knicks in 2006. Also, in 2006 the league adopted a dress code. I guess that meant no more bagging or sagging or you know what I mean, their ass hanging out. Well they might still wear those but at least a sport coat would cover it up. Also, in 2006 the Lakers and Minnesota wore a special patch in memory of George Mikan who I eluded to in my 1950's decade. So, did all of this excitement lead to larger crowds and higher television ratings? The answer is an emphatic not really. Attendance stayed between seventeen thousand per game in 2000 to seventeen thousand one hundred fifty in 2010. When reviewing television rankings, I took my information solely from the NBA finals played during the decade. The NBA was the same as baseball, the most fans and non-fans would watch the finals if they didn't watch any other games. Let me put this in a simple perspective for you. Prior to 2010 there were thirty-six years that the finals were televised. Of those thirty-six years, the decade between 2000 and 2010 produced seven of the worst viewer ratings in history. The 2007 Finals drew the lowest audience of all time with nine million viewers. Compare this to twenty-nine million viewers in 1998. Not good. Despite these numbers the league increased its salary cap to fifty-seven million dollars. Combine that with all the other expenses and what do we have once again? We have even higher ticket prices, even higher concession prices, higher memorabilia prices, higher parking passes. Fans were already unhappy...well you reap what you sow.

The NFL entered the decade riding a great high. As far as popularity was concerned the NFL was slowly replacing baseball as America's favorite sport. While fan interest peaked, the NFL followed suit with the other major sports when it came to off the field activity. Things went pretty well for the league until 2005 when it seemed all hell broke loose for the second half of the decade. In 2005 the Minnesota Vikings made headlines when seventeen members of the team were involved in the "love boat scandal". The event was named this after it was discovered that prostitutes were flown from Atlanta and Florida to entertain ninety guest on the boat. Four Vikings were charged with various crimes related to the incidents. The Vikings continued to have woes when they were later fined one hundred thousand dollars for Super Bowl ticket scalping. The decade came to a caving end for the Vikings when while being prepared for an upcoming game the roof collapsed on to the Metro Dome field. Luckily nobody was injured. The Vikings weren't the only team that were burdened by off field incidents. Following a Super Bowl winning season in 2007 New York Giants wide receiver Plaxico Burris accidentally shot himself in the thigh at a local nightclub. He was suspended and charged with procession of a handgun. If Burris thought his luck was bad, his world couldn't compare to that of Atlanta Falcon Quarterback Michael Vick. After being drafted as the first overall draft pick and going to three pro bowls, his career went to the dogs. No literally. He lost everything because of his dog kennel Bad News Kennels. It was bad news alright, bad for Vick and his dog fighting operations. He would eventually plead guilty to dog fighting and served almost two years in a federal prison. He came back in 2010 and made another Pro Bowl as a member of the Philadelphia Eagles. Vick filed for bankruptcy in 2008 but eventually paid all that he owed. There was also controversy on the field. It started in 2001 when Packers QB Brett Favre intentionally took a sack so that opposing defensive player Michael Strahan could break the most sacks in a season record. Now let me tell you that back in the day that (expletive) would never fly. The record stood but shouldn't have. Even the referees couldn't fly under the radar and they made their impression in the biggest game of the year. In the 2006 Super Bowl the Steelers defeated the Seattle Seahawks after which referees admitted to blowing three game changing plays giving the Steelers the title. The competition wasn't much better when for the first time in history a losing team made the playoffs with a losing seven win and nine loss record. While that wasn't good for the game there were many other firsts that stood out and provided fan interest despite all of the turmoil. 2006 was the first time that two African American head coaches made it to the Super Bowl. Tony Dungeys Colts would win. In 2002 Cowboys Emmitt Smith broke Walter Peyton's rushing record finishing his career with over eighteen thousand yards. Now let me put that in perspective for you. That is running ten and a half miles with eleven grown athletes trying to keep you from gaining any yards. In 2004 Colts Peyton Manning threw for forty-nine touchdown passes breaking Dan Marino's record. One of the most popular first of the decade was the founding of the NFL Network on cable TV. It had NFL action twenty-four hours a day three hundred sixty-five days a year. On game day they had one of my favorites, it was called Red Zone. RedZone would show plays from every game of the day and every single scoring play. At times they had eight games divided into one screen. The best part was no (expletive) commercials. None of that take this medicine for better sex, use this feminine hygiene product if you stink, drink these energy drinks so you can have a heart attack and best of all, if you take our prescribed medicine it could cause a hundred other things including death. Yea I was happy about RedZone. It remained a staple until the league shut down. In 2008 there was another distinct first in the decade. The Detroit Lions became the first and only team to lose all sixteen games.

The American Conference dominated the decade winning seven of the ten Super Bowls including three by the New England Patriots and two by the Steelers. How'd those Super Bowls translate into numbers. Super Bowls were watched by more viewers by far than any other decade. The decade produced nine of the top twenty-five most watched Super Bowls in history. I believe that Super Bowl viewership fails to tell the true story. How many people do you know that didn't watch an NFL game all season, can't name one player and probably doesn't know who's playing but they will have or attend Super Bowl parties? For the regular season the numbers fluctuated and by the end of the decade total viewership was up by a half of a percent from the previous decade. Fans in attendance also was up and down. For the first six years of the decade attendance gained each year. The following four years fans in attendance decreased each year. Still by the end of the decade attendance was up over eight hundred thousand fans for the decade. The NFL was in great shape entering the next decade and was now officially America's game. It should have stayed that way.

College football and basketball attendance and viewership stayed flat throughout the decade. That sounds like good news because there was no drop but the fact is that over the ten years the cost of everything continued to rise.

Riding the success of the previous decade the interest in soccer in the United States continued to grow as the number of teams, number of players, and number of fans increased at a rapid rate. Women's professional soccer began for the first time in 2001. Men's professional soccer also continued to thrive. Many credit the success of the men and women national teams for the new-found interest. The decade to follow would only provide more success for both national teams. In 2001 the Men's team qualified for its fourth straight World Cup, a record for the team. They clinched the berth in Foxboro Mass. in front of over forty thousand fans. That team would advance to the final eight for the first time since 1930. The men's team success continued into 2007 when they won their second Gold Cup in front of a packed stadium at Soldier Field in Chicago. While the men's team was knocking on the door of international success the women team was kicking it in! The women's team followed up its 1999 World Cup victory with another in 2003. The following year the U.S. women's team won every tournament that it entered including bringing home the Olympic gold medal. In 2008 the women team had its most successful year in history winning thirty three of thirty-four games and yet another Olympic gold medal.

In 2007 the United States introduced its youth to the newly formed U.S. Soccer Development Academy. An academy that wanted to develop youth players into national team players.

By 2006 there were twenty-four million Americans playing soccer. By 2010 over thirty percent of American households had at least one family member playing the sport of soccer. This was second only to baseball. By 2006 soccer overtook hockey as the nations forth most popular sport. In 2008 ESPN started to telecast Major League Soccer games. The sport was making all other sports step up and take notice. Salaries were not out of control. Ticket and concession prices were affordable to everyone. It was also a sport that could be played anywhere as long as you had a soccer ball.

Looking ahead to the next decade, you'll start getting a clearer picture of what happened to sports as we once knew it in America. No leagues will collapse but the groundwork will be laid for the disasters to come.

After finishing the article Beal sat in his chair, Manna poured him a glass of his shine. He thanked her and just smiled at the thought of opening day. He wondered if there would be any fans there to join him?

The following day, Joe Mills picked up Floyd Beal and met O'Leary at the office. The two friends signed the agreements and the two-million-dollar owner fees changed hands. The two longtime friends now owned the New York Empires! The two left the meetings and went to Big Uns. "That'll be two scoops of ice cream today", Beal told his friend. After all this was a celebration!

# Chapter XVIII

For the two months following the owner's meetings O'Leary, the owners and his dream team worked tirelessly to get the league off the ground. The owners voted to follow O'Leary's suggestion former major league commissioner would be commissioner of the new league. After all the failure of Major League Baseball was not the commissioner's fault. The groundwork for the eventual failure was laid decades earlier. Paul McGovern was voted President, Frank Riley Senior Vice President, and son Mike Riley was named executive Vice President. There were meetings held with the owners and with O' Leary's dream team. The first matter that had to be addressed was the draft. The draft would provide each team with twenty players and five extras in case of injuries. Each team would be allowed to draft fifty players and would then cut the team to twenty-five by opening day. The players would be ranked one through twenty-five so salaries could be determined and contracts signed. Since there was no college baseball the league would hold tryouts in all twelve cities and would conduct the draft in February 2030. Spring training would be held for the entire month of April. Spring training would be held in the team's home stadium to save on travel. O'Leary knew the state of Florida's economy took a hit when Major League Baseball folded and there was no more spring training held there, but he was in no position to help them out. His concerns were the financial success of the league and the return of professional baseball to America. Now that most relevant dates were set O'Leary could start visiting each city to see if there was anything he could do for the owners. He turned off the lights to his office and was finally heading for home. Abruptly he stopped turned the lights back on and returned to his desk. He'd forgot that new owner Floyd Beal's next article was published earlier in the day. He wanted to read it to see what he'd said about the new league and owning a team. He thought about his wife being home alone and changed his mind again. He needed to get home, she probably had a late dinner waiting on him. He'd told her numerous times over the years to hire a maid and a cook and a nanny when the kids were still at home. She always flatly refused any help. I can cook better than most, I can clean better than most, and I can certainly raise my children without the help of some stranger she'd always say. When he walked in the door he was shocked. The table was set, the lights were dim, and his favorite meal of Beef Wellington was on the table. "Why the special treatment?" he asked. "Oh nothing, it's just our anniversary" she answered. "Oh my God, it is! I am so sorry, I've been so busy. I promise I'll make it up to you". She accepted his apology but she was thinking. "When will you make it up to me after the new baseball league starts? Nope not then, there will be more work and travel than ever." Maybe someday she thought. O'Leary felt really bad. His wife had always been more than supportive. He knew it was time to slow down but he couldn't afford to at this point with the creation of the new league and the fight to bring back college sports. After dinner he forgot all about reading Beal's article and spent the evening losing yet another game of Scrabble to his wife. The following morning, he opened his laptop to read the article. He read:

In this article I will be describing many of the events transpiring this decade from 2010 through 2020 that led to the demise of professional and college sports in America. This decade did not actually produce any of the sports complete failures but there were many events during the ten-year span that would directly impact the future of all sports. It would also be a decade that would see the sport of soccer continue its rise in popularity. There was no decade in history that would provide such a decline in the interest of some sports nor has there been a decade when politics crept into sports like they did from 2010-2020. Anywhere politics creeps in, that it shouldn't, there's always trouble and the world of sports was no different.

All sports during this decade had lots of great moments and lots of negative influences that cost professional and college sports many of its fans. It started in 2010 when baseball great Mark McGwire admitted to using steroids including in 1998 when he broke Babe Ruth's record of 61 home runs in a season. This led to many other players being caught and punished. There was talk at the time that the records that were set by those using steroids should be abolished. Today the records still stand. Prior to that, the only time steroids were mentioned was at the Olympic Games or the Tour De France. During this decade they became illegal and a banned substance by all major sports. By now everybody wishes that steroids had been the worst obstacle facing professional and college sports. Sadly, that was just the beginning.

The National Football League had many issues between 2010 and 2020 that eventually would be significant in the demise of the league. Concussions, player flag protest, league rule changes, and loss of fan support all contributed to the eventual demise of the National Football League. The league spent over 600 million dollars over the decade to compensate former players for past concussion issues.

The league started taking measures in 2010 to better protect players from injuries and concussions. The league starting fining and suspending players for vicious hits and unnecessary roughness. The problem was those fines could not take back the vicious hits that resulted despite the fine.

There was a major study conducted about players receiving concussions during the period. These studies and conclusions led to the "concussion protocol" which was intended to protect players from serious injuries. There were multiple studies conducted that indicated nearly every NFL player suffered from CTE or Chronic Traumatic Encephalopathy. The disease caused by concussions causes memory loss, confusion, depression and dementia. A 2017 study indicated that ninety nine percent of brains donated by deceased NFL players and tested by scientist's indicated severe CTE. This study and the results continued to impact the rules of the game for years to come. These rule changes changed the face of the game and cost the league fans it could not afford to lose.

While the concussion issue was a big issue it wasn't the biggest concern that the NFL faced. The biggest issue that the NFL faced during this decade was players disrespect for the American flag. This caused attendance and season ticket sales to take a huge nose dive. The protests began in the NFL after San Francisco quarterback Colin Kaepernick sat and later knelled on one knee during the playing of the national anthem, as opposed to the tradition of standing, before his team's pre-season games of 2016. Throughout the 2016 season, members of various NFL and other sports teams engaged in similar silent protests. On September 24, 2017, the NFL protests became more widespread when over two hundred players sat or kneeled in response to President Trump's calling for owners to fire the protesting players. This led to many heated discussions between players and owners about how much control the owners had in response to the protest. The owners would eventually prevail and by the end of the 2017 season there were very few, if any, protesting players. As for the original protestor Colin Kaepernick things did not go well for him. In 2016 he opted out of a hundred and twenty-million-dollar contract in order to file for free agency. He did this unaware that no other NFL team would show interest in him due to his previous protest. He eventually lost eighty six million dollars by filing for free agency. Despite numerous efforts to prove that owners were colluding to keep him out of the NFL, this was never proven. Kaepernick would never play another down of NFL football. He never said as much but I believe Kaepernick regretted protesting. No proven good came out of the protest by any of the players. The protesting players stated they were protesting racism in America especially at the hands of the police. What protesting players failed to recognize was that the tradition of playing the National Anthem at most sporting events in America began in 1941. For seventy-five years every player stood in honor of America while the 198-year-old song played, that is until 2016. Colin K., the players that later joined in the protest, nor the NFL ever dreamed how much these acts would effect season ticket sales, single game ticket sales, concession sales, and team merchandise sales all declining sharply for years to come. The response of the fans was anger toward the players for disrespecting America. Fans burned jerseys, season tickets, and swore they'd never watch another game. By 2018 the owners were experiencing the loses in fans and income so they approved a rule that required all players to stand during the National Anthem or remain in the locker room. Players of the time failed to realize these owners asking them to stand for the national anthem not only signed their paychecks but also had every right to demand the players stand. As owners described the situation it was obvious there was no choice in the matter. They said that the NFL guideline stated that all players, coaches, and staff members would stand for the National Anthem. This to them was no different than a job description requiring an employee to wear a uniform, steel toed boots, or to clock in for work. Work place rules are put into place by employers and are to be followed by employees. The National Football League was no different. If players really wanted to make a difference they could take Monday through Saturday to try to make a real difference instead of disrespecting the American flag on Sunday. The players and the league learned this lesson the hard way. In 2017 and 2018 alone there were instances that led to large numbers of former fans walking away from the game. During the preseason of 2018 a New York Jets player knelt during the national anthem. The following week all New York City Police bonded and quit attending or watching NFL games. The fire departments soon followed. Restaurants stopped showing NFL games as did many bars. The results of these players actions was staggering at the gate.

From 2010 through 2017 the league averaged seventeen million plus fans per year. Keep in mind this number was the number of tickets sold and not the number of fans through the turnstiles. In 2018 following the abuse allegations, unpopular rules changes, and the players protest of the flag, the number of tickets sold dropped thirty percent down to just over eleven million tickets sold. The number of fans was even less with most stadium's half empty in 2018. The biggest cause for the drop was the drop in season ticket sales. In 2017 the average number of season ticket sales was eighty percent of the stadium's capacity. That number continued to drop. 2018 was a year that would define the early signs of an overall collapse. There were many indicators during 2018 that caused concern. The 2018 season began with the Washington Redskins fifty years of consecutive sellouts coming to an abrupt halt. One would think if the streak was going to end it would be because the team was performing poorly or facing an unpopular opponent. This was far from the true cause. The Redskins opened the 2018 season at home against division rival and defending Super Bowl Champion Philadelphia Eagles. The game drew less than sixty thousand fans compared to the previous seasons home opener against these same Eagles that drew a sellout crowd of eighty thousand. This was a drop of over thirty percent of attendance from one year to the next. The Washington Redskins did everything they could to get the fans back. They eliminated the waiting list for season tickets because there was nobody waiting anymore. The Redskins were not the only team with attendance issues, all of the league's teams suffered. The Tampa Bay Buccaneers in 2019 went as far as to give away tickets to attract fans and even this didn't fill the stadium. The league, networks, owners, and sponsors all hoped that even if the fans quit coming to the games they'd still watch the games on TV. They were disappointed. Viewer totals declined almost as much as fans through the turnstiles. There were a lot of different reasons for the decline in popularity but this writer believes it all came down to the issues with some players being viewed by fans as cry baby's or overpaid thugs. Why thugs? The definition of thug is " a violent person or criminal". Well that describes to a T the way the fans saw the players and there were good reasons. An All-Pro receiver for the New England Patriots was confirmed to be a gang member and was convicted of murder. He later committed suicide. A Kansas

City Chief murdered his girlfriend then drove to the Chiefs facility and killed himself. Teams were found to be offering players bounties for hurting an opponent's players. A Baltimore Raven All-Pro linebacker was caught on hotel video slugging his wife in the face with his fist. There were many players committing crimes and suicides attributed to brain damage suffered. Another was charged with conspiracy in two unsolved murders. An Atlanta Falcon All- Pro Quarterback was convicted of dog fighting. In 2017 before week two of the regular season there were headlines that read "How many scandals can the NFL possibly fit into one season?" I could go on and on and on about the scandals but if I had to name just one reason for the decline it would be the disrespect for the American flag.

By 2020 attendance had dropped to an all-time low of nine million and the number of season ticket holders had dropped by another thirty percent. The NFL saw it was in trouble and started making major changes by 2021 in hopes of saving the game and the league. Little did they know these changes would result in a continuous state of decline in attendance and television viewers.

The decade was much the same for Major League Baseball (MLB) as attendance dropped and television audiences decreased year by year until they reached an all-time low in 2020. Unlike the NFL there were few instances of domestic violence with the players, very few scandals, very few rule changes, so why the drastic drop and disenchantment with America's past time? The answer to this question is complicated. There were issues with the pace of play. The average time it took for a major league game rose significantly over the decades. In the twenties the average time for a nine inning major league game was one hour and forty seven minutes. By 2020 the time it took to complete a nine inning game was three hours and fifteen minutes. Much of this was due to media commercial breaks, multiple trips by the manager to the pitching mound and pitching changes by the manager. Fans were not thrilled with the increases in time or the overall ball park experience. As one fan explained there were other issues; You can "ditto the below to include NFL and NBA games also. I had never looked at it from his perspective but no words ever rang truer. The fan said "I leave my house at four thirty in order to drive into downtown for a seven o'clock game. It takes me thirty minutes to park. It takes me another forty five minutes to get through security and into the stadium. By now its six thirty. I find the nearest concession stand to my seat and pay fourteen dollars for a super footlong hotdog, ten more for french fries and sixteen for a super-sized beer. That is forty dollars I spent on a hotdog, fries and a beer or soft drink. That is a hundred and sixty for a family of four. That is on top of a hundred dollars for an upper deck seat while the stadium is well over half empty. So, me personally I have a hundred and forty dollars invested in the game. That family of four has over five hundred dollars spent for this night out. How many games do the owners think I can afford to come to in a year ? How many games can that family of four or more come to? After spending all that money, I still have to walk down forty steep steps to an empty area of seats. If I want to go to the restroom that's another forty steps down and forty steps up after waiting fifteen minutes to use the restroom. Before going back to my seat in the third inning I stop for another beer and a pack of peanuts. There's another twenty five so now I'm up to over a hundred and sixty dollars. Two and a half hours and another beer later the game finally ends. I make my way down the forty steep steps, make my way to my car. I then set still for almost an hour before leaving the parking lot. I drive the thirty minute drive home and arrive back at home at midnight. So, I spent close to two hundred dollars and almost eight hours of my time to witness a blow-out loss by the home team. Now let me tell you how most fans watch the game in 2020. That family of four buys two packs of Oscar Myer wieners and buns for ten dollars. They buy a bag of charcoal, a twelve pack of soda and a case of beer for twenty dollars. They even buy a bag of peanuts and a bag of popcorn. So, they have zero invested in tickets, less than forty in food and drink, don't have to walk up or down any steps to go to the restroom and can turn the game off at any point in the game. They also don't have to use eight hours to do it all. If they watch the whole game it will be a little over three hours. Die-hard fans counter with the quote "but you miss the game experience". Well in my opinion there's not much to miss." This fan's take on the game and attending the live ones has become the rule and not the exception. By 2020 attendance plunged by over thirteen million fans. In 2018 attendance fell below seventy million for the first time in fifteen years. This meant that eighty thousand less fans attended daily or over three thousand less fans every day in every stadium. That equates to an income loss of twelve million dollars per day. It became obvious that attendance was based on the successes of the teams. If you win, you have more fans. That is why baseball had to make many changes to keep America's game and Major League Baseball alive. Over the next decade they used the most innovative ideas to try and put fans back in the seats.

From 2010-2020 the National Basketball Association (NBA) was able to maintain a fan base despite issues the league faced. Some thought the decade was a good one for the NBA but most tired of the Cleveland Cavs and Lebron James verses Golden State and its all-star studded top to bottom team. Fans watched this matchup year after year until 2018 when the Warriors swept the Cavs four games to none. This all changed in 2019 when Lebron James joined the Los Angeles Lakers in hopes of bringing equality to the league. This move brought no equality to the league. The race to build a super team provided the fans with great NBA action but all the while attendance and overall interest continued to decline. The mindset of the majority of fans became that if they didn't live in Golden State or wherever Lebron James was, there was no need to waste their time. Why follow a team if you know there's no chance they go all the way and win a title? Do you really think Charlotte, Atlanta, Memphis, or any other small market really had a chance to win an NBA title? The answer is in the history books. The last small market team to win an NBA title was in 1979 when the Seattle Super Sonics took home the title. One champion year after year was not a recipe for success for the league. During this decade the "Super Teams" became the new trend. This all began in 2010 when Lebron James one of the best players in history left Cleveland for Miami in pursuit of an NBA championship. He talked a couple of other elite free agents into joining him in Miami. Together they won two NBA titles. This super team idea led to the formation of another super team the Golden State Warriors. This team would dominate the decade with five consecutive NBA finals appearances leading to them winning three titles led by five superstars that made up this super team. The NBA salary cap was supposed to prevent such super teams from being possible, but some way, somehow the owners found ways to manipulate the system. While this seemed like a great idea to the super team and its fan base but it was detrimental to the league as a whole. Why would fans of the other twenty nine teams pay to see or watch their home team that's playing for second at best? Every year it came down to the Golden State Warriors and whoever Lebron James was playing for. It started after James returned from Miami to join another Super Team in Cleveland. After losing to the Warriors year after year he left for the Los Angeles Lakers for his third super team and won his fourth NBA title in 2020 playing in the "Bubble" at Disney World in Orlando. By 2020 America was bored with the NBA and attendance and television ratings showed the decline. Even the opposing players and owners griped about the situation. In 2017 Michael Jordan, the greatest player of all time and owner of the Charlotte Hornets told the Washington Post: "You're starting to see a little bit of it now, where the stars are starting to gang up and go on one team," Jordan said in an interview for the 25th anniversary of the magazine. "I think it's going to hurt the overall aspect of the league from a competitive standpoint. You're going to have one or two teams that are going to be great and another 28 teams that are going to be garbage. Or they're going to have a tough time surviving in the business environment. From 2010 through 2018 attendance never reached twenty two million and never fell below twenty one million. By 2020 that number was reduced to nineteen million and would continue to decline at a rapid pace.

NCAA college sports took the greatest whipping of all sports other than Nascar racing between 2010 and 2020. There were so many issues during this decade that it could be a stand-alone yearlong article but I have to start somewhere. While there were many scandals already mentioned in previous decades, the decade between 2010-2020 was by far the most damaging to the NCAA, its college members, and intercollegiate sports itself. While previous scandals had damaged the reputation and integrity of the system nothing damaged it as much as the Penn State, Jerry Sandusky case. The Penn State sex scandal started with Jerry Sandusky an assistant coach for the Penn State football team, engaging in sexual abuse of children over a period of at least 15 years. Sandusky had located and groomed victims through his charity organization. The scandal broke in early November 2011 when Sandusky was indicted on 52 counts of child molestation. This scandal rocked the nation and the NCAA. Also, in 2011 the University of Miami football and basketball programs were both implicated in a scandal when a former booster was charged with providing improper benefits to the football and basketball players and coaches. Then there was the University of North Carolina scandal. in a follow-up to the UNC football scandal from 2009, new accusations of academic fraud arose in relation to the university's African and Afro-American Studies department and men's basketball program, men's football team, women's soccer and other sports as well. The Wainstein Report, an independent report commissioned by UNC, revealed academic fraud that occurred over at least 18 years involving thousands of students and student athletes. Allegedly, thousands of student athletes were directed by the UNC administration to take "sham" classes in order to maintain eligibility. UNC avoided major NCAA penalties, mainly because said sham classes had been offered to the entire student body. This event led many to believe that the NCAA was powerless and purposeless.

In 2015 staff members from the University of Louisville were accused of hiring a self-described former madam. She alleged that she had been paid several thousand dollars by a men's basketball staffer for strip shows and sex parties for players and prospective recruits. The NCAA announced the results of its investigation in June 2017, announcing major sanctions that included the loss of the team's 2013 national title. An appeal by Louisville failed, and in February 2018 the Cardinals became the first Division I basketball program to be stripped of a national championship. This not only cost the college a tremendous amount in fines and revenue losses but also cost coach Rick Pitino his job despite his denials of any knowledge of the events. While these events seemed bad enough the illegal activities to come made these acts look like child's play.

What would later become known as the NCAA basketball scandal of 2018 was a corruption scandal, initially involving sportswear manufacturer Adidas as well as several college basketball programs associated with the brand but eventually would involve many programs not affiliated with Adidas.

In September 2017, the FBI arrested 10 individuals, including four assistant coaches and an Adidas executive, on various corruption and fraud charges including bribery, money laundering, and wire fraud. The schools implicated in the initial announcement were Arizona, Auburn, Louisville (again), Miami, Oklahoma State, South Carolina, and University of Southern Cal.

The investigation then spread beyond the individuals and teams initially implicated. Within several months multiple media reports indicated that the Elite Youth Basketball League, the grassroots basketball division of Nike, was served with a subpoena by federal investigators. While Nike was not named in the initial documents, one of the 10 individuals arrested on September 26 was a former Nike executive who was working for Adidas when he was arrested.

The top revenue producer was college football. College football generated nearly seventy percent of overall college athletic revenue. In 2017 the average college football program generated more than thirty million dollars. All of the other sports combined raised less than half of that amount in revenue. It was easy to see that losing football would all but eliminate all the other sports. In February 2018 it was reported that college football attendance was the lowest it'd been in thirty six years with an average of forty thousand fans per game. The following season saw attendance drop for the fifth consecutive year, the only time that had happened in the history of the sport. The 2019 National Championship game between perennial powers Alabama and Clemson reported the lowest attendance in the history of national title games. The reductions would not only effect the basketball programs but the lost income would impact the other non-revenue sports including most of the women's programs. By 2020 nobody could have dreamed how much those facts would impact college sports in the future. With the sport of college football also losing fans at an incredible rate it was almost impossible for universities to maintain the other sports that depended on the football and basketball teams to shoulder the cost of the other sports.

To sum up the world of sports between 2010 and 2020 it was a time of the good, the bad, the ugly, and the outrageous. The good included great Super Bowls most involving Tom Brady and Bill Belichick's New England Patriots. Although it seemed like with every Super Bowl victory there was going to be a cheating conspiracy. Most of them, in my opinion, were just a case of Belichick outsmarting the other guys and that pissed them off. Who has spy planes fly over the opponent's practices? Bill Belichick. Who deflates the footballs so they are easier to throw in freezing temperatures? Coach Bill Belechek. Who by 2020 had been to nine Super Bowls and won six titles, Coach Bill Belichick. The dynasty known as the New England Patriots would fall early the next decade but we'll get to that in my next installment.

We also had great World Series during the decade, with two great oddities. The San Francisco Giants won three World Series during the decade. These were the first titles for the Giants since moving to San Francisco from New York in 1958. More startling is the fact that the New York Yankees won none. No world titles for the Yankees? This would be only the second decade in history that the Yankees failed to capture a World Series title. To put that number into perspective, that's a period spanning twelve decades. But all was not well with major league baseball either.

While Nascar, the NFL, NBA, MLB and college sports were suffering by the end of 2020, the National Hockey League (NHL), Professional Golfers Association (PGA), Professional Tennis, boxing, and even fake wrestling continued to keep its head above water during the decade not only in the United States but all over the world. While these sports thrived, it was the sport of soccer that continued to capture America's hearts. There was a period during this decade that many sports fans were captivated by the Men's and Women's World Cup and this was the only time they watched soccer. By 2016 the Premier League and the English Soccer League had caught fire in America and was one of the most watched sports. By 2018 the United States had Major League Soccer, North American Soccer League, United Soccer League, Premier League, and National Premier Soccer League. The National Premier League alone had ninety eight teams located nationwide and drew unbelievable crowds to their games. In 2018 the Major League Soccer attendance had increased by nearly sixty percent over an eight year period. The 2018 MSL Cup Final drew a record crowd of over seventy thousand. The following year it was over a hundred thousand breaking the overall attendance of any NFL Super Bowl in history. Both men's and women U.S. National teams gained in popularity. There was even an article printed in USA Today newspaper in July of 2018 questioning if soccer would soon replace baseball as America's most popular sport. The answer to that was an undeniable resounding yes!

# Chapter XIX

O'Leary was a little sad that Beal hadn't mentioned the new league or his ownership of the franchise in his article. Then he realized, Beal had only promised to write about the league in one of his articles and he still wasn't finished with the series so maybe the new league would get a mention in the following article. O'Leary decided he'd just stay at the office that night. It was already after midnight and he had a three thousand square foot condo attached to his office. It wasn't like he'd be uncomfortable. O'Leary poured himself a beer and opened the Demise to the next chapter. He figured the more he learned about why the other leagues had failed, the more successful he could make the American Baseball League. He started reading:

The National Football League suffered the previous decade from 2010 to 2020 with teams caught cheating, multiple cases of domestic violence, multiple players convicted of murder, or being murdered, along with numerous cases of suicide. Yet despite these events the biggest concern of the league was still concussions to players. The problem had become so widespread that parents were afraid to let their children play football. A measure was passed in the senate in 2023 that made it illegal for anyone under the age of sixteen to play tackle football. While the number of high school football teams in America had decreased by thirty five percent over a five year period, that was just the beginning. In 2023 the NFL itself changed rules, made equipment changes, and overhauled the game. The rule changes included the elimination of kickoff and punt returns. The ball was still kicked and punted. Where the "catcher", a newly created position, caught the ball or where the ball stopped indicated where the offensive team would take control of the ball. These rule changes eliminated the onside kick, eliminated the blocked punt, and eliminated the punt and kickoff returns that in the past could be game changers and some of the most exciting plays for the fans. Another new rule prevented a player from touching another player while he was airborne. Finally, players could not lower their head for any reason. The rule changes did not set well with the fans and attendance indicated such. The NFL was already trying to recover fans they lost during the eight year battle over the National Anthem and players rights to stand or not. This didn't help the recovery any as attendance continued to decline and by the midpoint of the decade only twenty four of the thirty teams remained in the NFL. Small market teams like the Carolina Panthers, Tennessee Titans, and New Orleans Saints could no longer compete on or off the field and thus folded. In the past there would have been other cities jumping at the possibility of having a professional football team relocate to their city but that was no longer the case. The rule changes in 2023 only spurned future decline in interest and Americans found other avenues to spend recreational dollars on. Player salaries dropped to that of the 1970's just because there was not enough income to pay the exorbitant salaries of the previous three decades. The biggest hit the league took was from television revenue a number that was cut by seventy five percent from 2016 to 2026 making it impossible for small market teams to compete for championships or be profitable. Another study was conducted in 2024 to determine the success of the rule changes in preventing concussions. The brain study was based on the brains of thirty players who had played under the new rules. The results were staggering. Ninety five percent of the players still had severe CPD. By 2026 the NFL decreased to sixteen teams all in major markets and no city had more than one team. Not even New York could support two teams and thus the old American Football League Jets folded. By the following year there was rumors that the leagues numbers attendance and viewership numbers had decreased drastically to the lowest numbers in over fifty years causing all major networks to drop the sport. ESPN and the NFL Network finally put together a deal that that would show three games a week on Sunday afternoon and Monday nights allowing the league the funds to operate for another season. Teams started selling tickets for five and ten dollars and season tickets for thousands percent lower than a decade prior. On July 4, 2027 the league called for a national news conference to be held at the Football Hall of Fame in Canton Ohio. NFL Commissioner Roger Goodell approached the podium to an outpouring of boos and heckles. Goddell was in his twenty first year as commissioner. He had been popular among owners but had never been popular among fans. He was accustomed to the boos. He'd heard them for twenty one years at the NFL draft. Today would be different. Goodell had worked for years with the owners to put together a product the fans would love. He approached the podium surrounded by hundreds of microphones. This was a hastily called news conference and the media expected the worse. That is exactly what they got. " Goodell couldn't start the news conference due the continuous booing. Every time he started to speak the thousands of fans denied him the opportunity to speak expecting the worse. "Good afternoon to our media and fans. Today is one of the most difficult of my life. I have loved the NFL since I was a kid. I have never been prouder to be a part of anything as I am to have served the NFL for the past twenty one years. Over the past ten years the NFL has suffered from the loss of high school and college football. We have suffered from the physical and emotional damage cause by concussions. This despite an all-out effort to make the game as safe as possible. Test data shows we failed in this aspect. Over the decades, players got bigger and stronger and no helmet could be developed to keep up with the size and strength of the current players. From 1997-2027 players average size was three inches taller and forty pounds heavier. Add to this strength increased by thirty three percent. Helmets and pads can only be made so safe. The next big obstacle to overcome was the flag protests starting in 2016 with Mr. Kaepernick knelling during the National Anthem. I

am going to post on the screen behind me the typical emails our office
was receiving from former fans. The first email said:

"Dear Pittsburgh Steelers and the NFL: I want to thank you for
freeing up my Sundays. Some of the earliest memories of my
life are watching Steelers games with my dad. I was once a sea-
son-ticket holder. I have occasionally missed a few games on
TV through the years due to scheduling conflicts, but I can
honestly say in my 44 years of living, I have never intentionally turned off a Steelers game. That changed today. As I sat
down to watch the Steelers-Bears game today, I learned from
the sideline reporter that the Steelers chose not to participate
in the national anthem. I realize that there is a lot of injustice in
our country. I realize that there are a lot of people upset at the
current administration. I realize that we live in a free country
where people have the freedom to not participate in the national
anthem. I also have the freedom to not spend another minute
or dollar on your product. I am of the opinion that this is quite
possibly the worst way to go about "protesting." If you want to
hold a rally at Heinz Field to allow your players to voice their
opinions, that would be fine. If you want all the Steelers and
NFL players to march on Washington D.C., fine. But to not participate in the national anthem is an insult to every serviceman
who has served or has passed away defending this country. If
you are truly that unhappy with the country, feel free to play
for the CFL. So, thank you, Steelers and NFL, for freeing up my
Sundays. I will no longer waste my time or money watching
your product. The weather today the in Pittsburgh area is beau-
tiful and I cannot think of a better day to spend it outside, away
from the TV. — **Jim Coletti**"

I'll allow a few minutes for you to ingest this before we continue.
Boos continued to erupt but it was obvious the commissioner had

gained everyone's attention. "OK here's another to educate you: " Sonny Jurgensen was my favorite player growing up, so you can tell I've been watching the NFL for a while. Watched as Billy Kilmer and his wobbly passes replaced him and didn't miss a beat. Great time to be a football fan. Now politics has reared its ugly head and crept into the game. This whole country has gone crazy. Maybe it was escapism, but it was nice to be able to watch without any of that in the game. I know there is a lot of social injustice in the world and the USA might lead the way in this, but it was nice to be able to watch a game without any of this involved.

Yesterday was the first Sunday I didn't watch a minute of football since before Nixon. Don't plan on watching any more. Which really hurts, since I've been a Falcons fan since they drafted Tommy Nobis. If this is what football has come to, stick a fork in me, because I'm done.

Goodell continued" I could put hundreds of thousands of emails similar to these but I don't want to waste your time. The bottom line is that the flag protest was the first giant step toward losing our fans. Fans were Americans first and fans second." It was clear to everyone in attendance that NFL fans even the hard core ones would support their country over overpaid, spoiled, protesting players. The Commissioner continued " If politics wasn't enough of a hill to climb, the league was faced with 2020 and Covid-19. This virus was something that took the nation and the NFL by storm. At the time the public was aware of the impact it took on individuals, the travel industry, restaurants, and bars, they always overlooked the impact it had on our already fragile league. There would be no draft, there would be a limited training camp, there would be no preseason games. The regular season attendance in 2020 would include the fact that half of the league had zero attendance for the season. The other half of the league averaged less than ten thousand fans per game. Lack of fans translated once again to lost revenue from ticket sales, parking receipts, concession sales and memorabilia sales. There was no way that the reduced television revenue could compensate for those huge losses. The next obstacle that we could not overcome was the test results from the concussion testing, we cannot justify to our players the choice of playing and chancing permanent brain damage or not. Finally, there is the truth that the current generation is not nearly as interested in sports as those of past generations. There are many things that occupy their time but the fact is the interest in not only the NFL but all sports has declined. All of those facts lead me to the purpose of this news conference. Today we announce the end of the National Football League. The owners and I have discussed every option. From starting a professional flag football league, to reducing the teams to eight. Nothing can keep this very proud league from folding. The fan base is just no longer there". The boos echoed for over five minutes. It was obvious that the only true fans left of the NFL were in attendance on this day. The commissioner was ready to take questions from the same media that'd covered the NFL during the successful years and witnessed the demise. First question 'You mentioned many reasons for the demise of the NFL. If you had to choose one, what is the main reason that the NFL folded?" The commissioner responded " If you ask a hundred fans you'd get a hundred different answers. I honestly believe that the lack of interest in the sport by the current generation was the number one cause" he responded. "So, you don't believe that the health of the players was the number one concern? " No there have always been injury concerns from the time that the NFL began. There were changes made throughout the history of the NFL to protect players. Remember we started out with leather head covers and no leg pads. We advanced to pads to protect every part of the body including scientific designed helmets to protect the brain". A reporter near the back responded "well there wasn't much success". "No" the commissioner responded "but we did the best we could possibly do to insure the safety of our players." "Was the demise politically motivated due to player protest"? Goddell responded " I can't be, what's the term, politically correct? Of course, it did. When lifelong fans burn jerseys, season tickets, and team flags, and write letters saying they are third generation lifelong fans that in an instance lost all interest speaks for itself." The next writer responded "so this is Kaepernick's fault? He destroyed the NFL"? "Goodell angrily responded " I said earlier that many factors weighed in on the demise of the National Football League. Whether it be concussions, no college football, protest and politics, or a lack of interest in any sports by the current generation, the fact is the NFL can no longer survive. It is with great sadness that today I have to announce that the NFL has come to an end, all teams and the league itself will be filing bankruptcy and admit defeat.

On that fourth of July I realized that America had lost yet another professional sport. What was to come? Or should I ask?

O'Leary wasn't tired yet so he poured himself another beer and continued to read Mills book.

# Chapter XX

Throughout the writing of the Demise I have stuck to each individual sport, its demise, the causes, all while trying to determine who was really to blame if any one person or any one thing. In the sports discussed up to this point, there were many reasons and many people to blame. I feel like it's important to dedicate this chapter not to a certain decade or a certain sport but to a particular year. For many it would be a far-fetched idea to think that one year caused the decline of major professional and college sports in America. That would be a far-fetched idea. What wouldn't be a far-fetched idea is that these sports were already having issues with attendance, television ratings, political issues, and 2020 would be the year that would start the fall over the cliff. It all started in early January 2020 when the World Health Organization announced the virus Covid-19 in China. January 21st the first case was confirmed in the United States. By March the virus was declared a Pandemic. Now I'm not going into the details of the virus only to say that it divided America and it dismantled the world of sports as we knew it and sports in our country never fully recovered from 2020. If the pandemic and already existing political issues weren't enough police brutality against blacks became national news when numerous black men and women were believed to have been murdered by police officers. This led to the national movement BLM standing for Black Lives Matter. So, the Covid-19 pandemic and the BLM combined to upstage anything that teams on a court or field could possibly do. It's really hard to find a starting point on how 2020 effected the world of sports. Everyone agreed that 2020 was the worst year for sports in America since World War II. It was the first time there had been no

NCAA basketball tournament. All winter and spring sports were cancelled at the college level. Then the dam broke, all hell broke loose, and in a matter of weeks the world of sports in America would be changed forever. In March the National Basketball Association suspended its season indefinitely. The following day the Big Ten Conference, Atlantic Coast Conference, both cancelled the remaining games in their respective tournaments. This was followed by the cancellation of all remaining conference basketball tournaments. That same day the National Hockey League suspended its season, Major League Baseball cancelled spring training and would delay the start of the season. The NCAA cancelled its men's and women's basketball tournaments better known as March Madness. It was the first time there had been no NCAA basketball tournament since 1939. Later in the day, all winter and spring sports were cancelled at the college level. Thursday March 12, 2020 would come to be known as March Mayhem. On the following day, Friday the 13th, President Trump declared a national emergency. Later that morning Nascar races were cancelled, golf tournaments were cancelled, including the Masters tournament. On Saturday March 14th all three major sports Hall of Fames shut their doors. By Monday March 30th there were no sporting events being held in America or anywhere in the world. The Covid virus not only effected America's sports but also the worlds. On March 30 the International Olympic Committee canceled the Tokyo Olympics and moved the date to the summer of 2021. There was no soccer, baseball, football, basketball, golf, wrestling, hockey, racing, and no college or high school sports. For the first time in history there were no sports being played in America. There is much to be said about the negative influence Covid 19 had on the economy and on the attitudes of the American people but my intention is to examine the effects on the world of sports as we once knew it. Each league and every college conference attempted to rebound from the effects of the virus but all failed miserably. The NBA was the first to attempt a finish to the season. The season finally restarted in the "bubble" at the end of July. The top twenty two teams were invited to play eight additional regular season games to determine the playoff seedings. All games including the playoffs would be played inside Disney World of Sports in Orlando Florida. All players, family and staff were quarantined inside the bubble until their season ended. There were no fans allowed but all important regular season games and all playoff games were televised. A month later the season was suspended a second time due to a wildcat strike conducted by the players in response to racial injustice and deaths caused by police officers. Entire teams knelt. Players wore shirts with racial injustice slogans, and stars spoke out about not only the perceived racial injustice but also about their political views. The finals finally ended with Lebron James and the Lakers winning the title ending the longest season in history lasting one year and twelve days. Whether it was due to the Corona-19 virus, fans response to the players protests, or just an overall lack of interest, the popularity of the NBA was coming to an abrupt end. In games prior to the initial stoppage only two of thirty teams averaged as many fans in attendance as the previous year. Television ratings were even worse yet. Months before the pandemic or the protest the NBA Saturday Premier game featured the Lakers and the Houston Rockets. The game was viewed by fourteen percent less viewers than the previous year and viewership dropped by nearly forty percent from two years prior. Worse yet the number of viewers for the playoffs dropped even more. The playoffs were viewed by thirty seven percent less fans than the previous season. The Finals were watched by nearly fifty percent less viewers than the previous season. Despite the numbers showing a huge decline in fans in attendance, viewers, and a loss of revenue due to no fans being allowed in the games, the league continued to spend like it was in its heyday.

Major League Baseball was effected as well. The start of the regular season was delayed by almost three months and before the end of the first weekend of play in July there were already games being cancelled. Games were continually postponed on a daily basis. No fans were allowed and much like the NBA, MLB viewership took a turn for the red. The Division championship series viewership dropped by over forty percent from the previous season. The World Series was the least watched in the history of televised World Series.

College sports would resume in the fall of 2020. College football games were played in empty or nearly empty stadiums with piped in fan noise and reaction. It became comical at times when the home team scored a touchdown and got booed due to a sound malfunction. College basketball would also return as scheduled with no fans in attendance and everyone who wasn't playing wore a face mask. The NFL also kicked off as scheduled without any preseason games. Every week of the season games were cancelled, moved, or rescheduled due to positive Corona-19 tests.

The events of that year ravaged the already fragile world of sports in America. There started to be articles written, television shows, and sport analyst that started predicting that it may cause the end of sports as we knew it. They could have not been more correct in their predictions than if they'd have been Nostradamus himself.

O'Leary closed his computer and headed to bed. It'd been a long day.

As time passed O'Leary continued to form relationships with new owners, he enjoyed viewing the new team logos, and negotiating deals that would meet the financial needs of the league.

Ron Mills and Floyd Beal continued to meet at Floyd's house on a daily basis planning for the draft, evaluating players and possible manager candidates. Due to the decline in Floyd Beal's health and the three day turnover between articles, Ron sat down with him and helped him with the next article. Manna didn't say a word but she was relieved and happy for Mills assistance with the article. She'd learned more about sports in the past six months than she ever imagined she could learn, or ever wanted to learn. For her it wasn't an enjoyable experience. She'd rather spend her time reading recipes and foraging books or watching reruns of Columbo. The two friends completed the article just in time to meet the publishing deadline. Mills read it to Beal before presenting it to the editors.

Happy Thanksgiving everyone. Today is my eighty ninth Thanksgiving and it's my favorite holiday. I always made it a point that on every announcing contract I negotiated there was a clause that stated that I didn't work on Thanksgiving or Christmas. So, let's get this over with, turkey and dressing are waiting. The ten years between 2020-2030 is much more memorable to me. Not because it's only more recent history, but because of all of the significant changes the world of sports witnessed. While there was tremendous changes made throughout the world, the world of sports in America was turned upside down. In the sports world this became known as the beginning of what is now known as the "Dark Decade" when sports as we had known it for decades came to a crashing halt.

By 2020 all professional and college sports in America were experiencing issues with attendance drops, declining television ratings and an overall drop in the interest of sports overall. These were all issues that the different teams and leagues were working to overcome. Little did they know that in early 2020, those issues would be the least of their problems. In January there were rumors of a virus unknown to most Americans. The Corona-19 virus took America by storm and changed sports in America in a manner that had never been witnessed prior. .While the virus was discovered in the sixties in Brazil, it was unknown to Americans. It wouldn't be long before all Americans would become very aware and impacted by the Corona virus. By February 2020 there were only fifteen confirmed cases in America. A month later there were seventeen hundred confirmed cases including forty six deaths. By the end of April there were over one million confirmed cases. Panic hit America and the world of sports, not only nationwide but worldwide. Toilet paper, disinfectant cleaners, and face mask became difficult if not impossible to purchase. Later it would be be pork, eggs, and frozen pizzas that were flying off the shelves. Employers asked employees to work from home or not at all. Flights were cancelled and the number of flyers dropped by ninety percent. Cruise ships were docked and not allowed to enter port. All restaurants were closed except for delivery and carryout orders. People were forced to wear face mask and rubber gloves when they went into public. While that all seems extreme it pales in comparison to how sports was effected. In early March, the initial plan was for the NBA and the National Hockey League to play games without any fans in attendance. Fans were not happy about this but soon they would become a lot unhappier. By mid-March, the NBA, NHL, and Major League soccer league suspended all games and quarantined all players. In addition to these actions, the NCAA cancelled March Madness, the NCAA basketball tournament. The NCAA also cancelled all springs sports. For the first time in history there were no sports of any kind being played in the United States. The impact was felt all over the world. Overall things started to improve by June. The number of corona cases dropped nationwide and worldwide. Many countries started to reopen. The United States slowly reopened one state at a time. The reopening came in phases that concluded with everything getting as close to normal as possible after such a historical event. Well almost everything. If the world of sports in the United States wasn't effected enough by its previous political issues and then by the Corona-19 Virus, the worst was yet to come. The death of a black man, George Floyd, at the hands of the Minneapolis Police Department made as much impact on the sports world as it did the nation itself. Floyd died when a police officer knelt on Floyd's neck for over thirteen minutes causing his death. Protest in response to Floyds death and police brutality against black people in general quickly spread across the United States and internationally. The reaction of the sports world was much the same with players from all the major sports tweeting, making Facebook posts, leading protest, and reacting to the racial injustice much of the country felt during this already time of unrest. While the general population was protesting, tearing down confederate monuments and statues, looting and setting fires in their own communities, professional and college athletes were planning ways that they could help the cause. The only problem is that these actions came very late, many years too late. The controversial statements and proposed actions by the athletes also could not have come at a worse time with all the sports already facing a decline in fans and interest and revenues. Most importantly...revenues. Due to the Corona-19 Virus the NBA suspended its season in March. In June it was announced that the NBA would take the top 22 teams and put them in a "bubble" using Disney World in Orlando Florida as its "bubble". Players nor family members would not be allowed to leave the secluded area. To make a long story short, the bubble burst and we all know what happened to the NBA after that.

The National Football League followed suit with the perfect chain to demise. The demise started with increased ticket and concession prices in the 90's Kaepernick's protest, followed by the concussion issues, followed by player protest from 2010-2019, followed by Covid-19 in 2020, followed by continual loss of fan base and television revenue, followed eventually ending the NFL's run in 2027.

Major League baseball's woes also continued. The measures to cut length of games was unsuccessful. The owners lowered ticket prices, provided free parking, had half price concessions days, and made players more available to fans in hopes of increasing interest in the game and bring more fans to the ball park. As mentioned before, in 2018 MLB attendance dropped to its lowest mark in twenty one years with a little over sixty million tickets sold. Don't confuse this with the number of fans in the seats as that number was less than half of the tickets sold. By 2024 there were only twenty five million tickets sold and by 2027 the number had dipped to less than fifteen million tickets sold. Despite MLB eliminating another eight teams decreasing the number of teams to twenty the numbers continued to decline. The owners hoped that by eliminating so many teams that those teams' fans would go see other teams thus increasing the fan base. In 2026 the average number of fans buying tickets was at the four thousand mark with a forth of those fans not actually attending the games. The end was near.

College sports and the NCAA suffered even more than professional sports from 2020-2030. The biggest cause for concern was the loss of NCAA power and the loss of revenue associated with college athletic programs nationwide. It began with all of the crimes, violations, and controversy from the previous decade and these continued into 2020 and beyond. The negative media attention cost college sports many of its fans and failed to attract the younger fan base necessary to sustain college sports as it'd moved forward in past decades. The larger universities were still able to attract enough fans and revenue from football and basketball to support the other "minor" sports and women's sports. But that would eventually end. The amateur rule further complicated things when the Supreme Court ruled that college players could profit from their name and image without giving up their amateur status. This caused more issues in the quest for equality between men's and women's sports. Within the first two months of the ruling, ninety five percent of those signed to endorsement deals were male. Colleges athletic budgets were reduced drastically when fans were no longer able to attend games in person. There was lost ticket sales, parking fees, memorabilia sales, and concession sales. This forced Universities to start trimming budgets, eliminating various sports, both male and female. And we all know what that led to.

When I first started this series of articles I think readers thought I'd be a cantankerous, over opinionated, old geezer. For my next story, I am. I know I said earlier I wouldn't mention Nascar again but after much thought I decided to give you my opinion. Nascar, was the first of the major sports to fold in America. The reason is simple, easy as A-B-C or Arrogant Business Comrades. The leaders of the Comrades became greedy and arrogant forgetting what made Nascar successful to begin with. It wasn't the big city tracks or the huge sponsors. It wasn't making millions of dollars off of high priced tickets. It' wasn't ten dollar beers and eight dollar hot dogs. It was the closeness of the Nascar community and its fans. It was spending a blue collar family's two weeks of vacation away from the cotton mill traveling to see the races. It was bringing your own beer. It was bringing your own food and camp at the track for a week or sometimes two. Nascar had planned a full slate of races in 2025 but when the most popular race on the circuit drew less than ten thousand fans through the turnstile, in July 2024, they lost over five million dollars and Nascar immediately folded. Nascar President and former seven time Nascar points champion Jimmie Johnson joined Nascar's attorneys making the announcement in front of media representatives.

Nascar was born in the South supported by Southerners. You know the "Red Necks". Maybe it's not politically correct but at nearly ninety years of age who cares? The downfall started with the expansion of Nascar racing nationwide. Did the powers that be really think that a city like Chicago with the Bears, Black Hawks, Cubs, White Sox and Bulls would be excited about cars going around and around a track five hundred times? Did the powers that be really believe that visitors to the "sin city "as Vegas would take time away from their sin time to watch cars go around in a circle? Would all those folks in the Lone Star state care as much about cars going around a track as they did about watching bucking bulls, broncos, and BBQ? They would find out the answers to these questions was all the same, a big emphatic no. It wasn't a matter of racing no longer being popular. Just the opposite is true. Following Nascar folding, the short tracks in North Carolina, South Carolina, Georgia, Tennessee, and Alabama thrived like never before. There were lines out the ticket booths, fans tailgated with friends. Once inside concessions are cheap and the experience is fun again. There are no major sponsors just local garages, burger joints, and a doctor here and there sponsoring friends race cars. There are very few rules concerning the cars, pretty much the same ones that were followed in the sixties and seventies short track racing. The only former Nascar tracks still in use are in Darlington SC and Bristol TN. where champion drivers from all the local tracks in five states convene at the end of the year to determine the overall Southern Auto Association Champion. These races draw a capacity crowd of nearly sixty thousand annually. The rest of the tracks are less than a mile long and race on Friday and Saturday nights or Sunday afternoons. They each seat between eight and fifteen thousand fans. So, to sum up the hard cold facts, Nascar tried to expand and attract fans nationwide into areas that entertainment dollars were being spent on other sporting events or entertainment. Early on sponsors jumped on board, ticket prices and concessions increased, and early on the plan seemed to work. But it wasn't long before Nascar lost its true fan base and the next generations had no interest in automobile racing. This loss of interest led to the demise of professional drag racing and Indy style racing shortly after the collapse of Nascar.

Now we get to the major beneficiary of the failure of sports in America and the Covid-19 pandemic. Soccer, Futbol, whatever you want to call it came out of the decade as the most successful and watched sport in America and the world. This old man started thinking about how a sport that wasn't even offered in colleges until the late fifties and in high schools until the seventies would become the most popular sport in America. The sport stayed about tenth in popularity in the United States for many years. There were moments of popularity growth for the sport in the eighties, nineties, and on into the new century. Over the next twenty years the sport gained in popularity with the success of the men's and women's National teams and World Cup success. By 2020 nearly every high school and every college in America had both men's and women's soccer teams. By 2024 soccer was played by more people in the United States than any other sport. Today that popularity has only increased. With the demise of professional football, baseball, and basketball, and the elimination of college sports, soccer became the sport of choice. Why? How? Baseball, basketball and football were invented in America and all were failing, why was soccer so successful. Let's start with the obvious, finances. It's a very inexpensive game to play, all you need is a ball and a goal, hell the goals can be made of cardboard boxes. Uniforms? Tee shirts of the same color...and that's it. No pads, no helmets, no bats, no using twenty balls a game, no goalpost, no fences, well you get the point. Second reason? Everybody can play soccer, if you can kick a ball you can play soccer. You don't have to be seven feet tall or built like Hercules. Just how popular is soccer in the United States? The most popular sports league in America is the AFL or

American Futbol League consisting of twenty four teams, all in former NFL cities. It was founded in 2027 after the collapse of the National Football League. Average attendance is over sixty thousand per game and the league has profited every year since its inception. There are over twenty thousand youth leagues in America. Twenty thousand leagues equates to an estimated over one and a half million youth soccer players. While soccer was always the most popular worldwide, it's now the most popular in our country and the popularity increases daily.

I have really enjoyed recording these articles for all of you concerning the history of our great sports in America. While it's been a joy to be able to relive so many historical and exciting events I was fortunate enough to witness in my lifetime, it's also been extremely sad reliving the demise of sports as we came to know it and enjoy it our entire lives. On a more positive note, as you know there is a group of wonderful people working to bring professional baseball back to America. It will be different but in this case the changes give the new league the best chance of success. Now I'm ready to move on to my new position as co-owner of the New York Empires baseball team. I look forward to seeing you at the games as we bring professional baseball back to America!"

Shaun O'Leary was happy to see the new league got some publicity from Beal. The more support the league had from old timers, the better.

# Chapter XXI

Joe Mills told Bea goodbye and excitedly headed out the door to go to the final owners meeting before baseball would actually return to America. He was also excited to be picking up his friend and co-owner Floyd Beal. Mills had noticed a huge decline in Rocket's mental health since he'd finished the newspaper articles and bought the team. There had been several occasions when he'd had to make decisions for the new team because Beal wasn't capable. He pulled into Beal's driveway and was greeted by Manna. He gave her a tight hug and asked how Beal was doing. "He's doing great today. He got up this morning, ate breakfast, and knew you were coming to pick him up for a meeting. He couldn't remember what the meeting was about but he knew you were coming. Now yesterday he knew he was the owner of the Empires but thought they were still the Mets of old. Some days are good, some not so good." she finished. Floyd Beal came out wearing overhauls and a flannel shirt. She'd tried to get him to change but he wouldn't hear of it. Mills smiled, greeted his friend and told her, "He looks fine". Beal smiled at her and said "told you so"! She just laughed and shook her head.

Shaun O'Leary walked into his office for the final owners' meetings on April 27,2030 with the season's first pitch only a month away. At the meeting O'Leary's Dream Team was in attendance along with team owners, executives, and select members of the media. O'Leary walked to the podium, pumped both fist in the air and shouted into the microphone "We did it"!! "We did it" he exclaimed a second and a third time. Every person in attendance stood and gave a loud two minute standing ovation. O'Leary's eyes welled with tears as what seemed like an impossibility only months ago was actually coming to fruition. He dried his eyes and started the meeting. " I am here today to give everyone a final update on the successful formation of the All American Baseball League.

Per the schedule you received I will address each topic separately and in order. Most of you are fully aware of everything I am going to say but I want to make sure we are all on the same page. Please hold any questions until the end.

Finances : I know everyone wants to know how the finances of the league are going since that was one of the major issues in the past failures. Finances are excellent. The plan to rent and not own stadiums has helped decrease cost tremendously. By lowering executive salaries, umpire salaries, coaches and player salaries we have in turn been able to lower ticket prices, parking prices, concessions, and memorabilia prices so that more fans can enjoy the game. Later in the meeting you'll be able to see just how much this has helped. So financially we are in A plus shape.

Next on our agenda are the teams. Since we last met teams have hired what they needed to operate internally including a manager, a batting coach and a pitching coach. In late February and early March, the league held five West Coast tryouts and five East Coast tryouts attended by the three coaches from each team. Tryouts were attended by over two thousand potential players. Teams were then allowed to invite up to fifty players to their home fields for further evaluation. The enthusiasm of the potential players was way beyond our expectations. I wondered if we'd be able to draw quality players to the league with our salary ladder pay scale. In the end my initial thought proved correct. Players play a sport because they love the game. They would rather make a minimum fifty thousand dollars per season plus bonuses playing a game they love rather than work a nine to five office job or selling something they don't even like. On Monday March 26th the All American Baseball League held its first ever draft. Every team selected fifty players. From this pool, each team signed twenty five players who were signed to contracts based on player ranking one through twenty five. There was also a pool of five players per team in case of injuries. Final rosters will be released to the media for the first time following this meeting. I think what will surprise the media and the fans the most is the number of former major league players that will adorn the rosters. While most of the former league's stars were able to find work in other countries, there were many that couldn't get a contract or didn't want to move to a foreign country to continue their careers. Of the three hundred players signed for opening day rosters, two hundred sixty five are former major league players. Many of these players went from making millions a year four years earlier to making a hundred thousand per year. It was still better than most of the jobs the players had been able to obtain since the league folded. Teams will hold a two week spring training held in their own stadiums to control cost. There will be no spring training games in this initial season. The season will begin on Friday May twenty forth which is Memorial Day weekend. Games will be played on Friday night, Saturday night, and Sunday afternoon. Single game tickets for all games will go on sale tonight at midnight." O'Leary stopped in mid-sentence, he turned around and walked toward a tall lean man dressed in a black suit and sunglasses. The man handed O'Leary an envelope and walked away. No words were exchanged. He returned to the podium. "I apologize for the delay but these are the first two week results of season ticket sales for all of your teams. I have no idea what's in this envelope. Ticket Tracker has been in charge of all sales and these are the first results. We will hope for the best but take into consideration that fans don't even know who's on their teams yet. Memorabilia with new logos have not been released yet nor have the schedules." O'Leary opened the envelope to find twelve smaller envelopes. "OK here we go. These numbers are as of last night at midnight. Each team had ten thousand season tickets to sell. If they could just sell a quarter of those, the league would be in tremendous financial shape entering the initial season. O'Leary's hands started to shake and he started to sweat as he struggled to tear open the first envelope. "We'll start with the East. "Boston you have sold,", he stopped, looked down at the sheet of figures, shook his head and continued " Boston you've sold ten thousand season tickets. Your sold out"! The entire room broke out in applause. " New York Big Apples, you too are sold out!" He opened the envelopes and Mills prepared for the worst. Could New York possibly support two teams? "Empires you are also sold out with ten thousand season tickets sold"! Mills couldn't contain himself, he started to hug his friend when he realized that Floyd Beal was sleeping. O'Leary continued down the list of teams finally getting to team number twelve the Texas Cowpokes. "Texas you are the twelfth team that I am happy to say has sold out of season tickets" ! He pumped his fist in the air, everyone in the room was celebrating, and congratulating one another. Mills knew he should be celebrating too but it was time to take his friend home. He walked Floyd Beal to his car and headed for his old friend's house. "That was a good meeting" Beal said. "Yes, it was" Mills replied.

The meeting continued without the two Empire owners. O'Leary waited until the room full of people were done celebrating. " I'll see each of you on opening weekend, one month from today" Congratulations to all of you on a job well done. " Over the next four weeks O'Leary was involved in making sure everything was ready for opening day. While this took up the majority of his time he spent every extra minute lobbying anyone who would listen to approve his injunction allowing for college sports to return. This was a project he'd began long before his idea to bring back baseball. While his baseball idea moved quickly, his lawsuit moved slowly. He'd say it was because he didn't have to type thousands of papers and complete case studies to start a new baseball league.

During those next three weeks following the meeting Mills made it a point to visit Rocket Beal daily. Beal still had good days but the bad days started to be more of the norm. At one of the visits Manna surprised Mills when she told him that Beal hadn't really came up with the all of the facts for the articles on his own. He didn't really remember all of those events he talked about so she'd look up the facts and have him talk about them. He still had a good enough mind that when reminded of certain games or players, he could still voice his own opinions. It was still his ideas she explained but he just needed a little memory jog-gling along the way. Joe hoped that his friend would have a good day on opening day and be able to attend the opening ceremonies. A cal-endar hung in his kitchen and some days he'd remember to mark off the days until opening day and sometimes he wouldn't. During this time the league had become a favorite of the media and everyone seemed excited to welcome professional baseball back to America. Now it was mere days before its return.

Joe Mills and his wife went to pick up Floyd Beal and his Manna on Friday around three in the afternoon. She met them at the car and Joe expected the worst. Wasn't Beal able to go? Had he passed away"? His concern turned to laughter when out came Floyd Rocket Beal in his overhauls and flannel shirt singing take me out to the ball game as loud as he could. "He's been doing that all morning. Don't worry he's well aware of who he is and what's happening today." she said. "Damn right I know who I am, why wouldn't I? I'm Floyd Beal and I'm going to announce tonight's game". "Uh oh" Joe thought. Just kidding, just kidding Beal laughed.

The first game for the Empires was against the cross town rival Big Apples. When they arrived at the stadium there was already a line of fans waiting to enter the stadium. In the parking lot were numerous signs stating there was Free Parking. This same parking four years ear-lier ranged from twenty to fifty dollars. The memorabilia stands were swamped with fans buying ten dollar hats that used to be twenty five. Fifteen dollar jerseys that used to be fifty dollars. It was a wonderful sight to see. The remainder of the afternoon went by quick and at five o'clock fans began to enter the stadium. The opening festivities would begin at six and the game started at seven. It wasn't long after the sta-dium opened that Mills began to realize this game was sold out. The fans were happy with the changes and anticipation was in the air along with the smell of hot dogs and popcorn. Joe Mills and the others settled into the owner's suite to watch the festivities. Floyd Beal took a look down at the field and asked "why the are hell we sitting up here? I saw this view for over forty years. I want to be on the field where I can smell the grass." Joe took Beal by the arm, led him out of the fancy owners' box, took him into the home team dugout and sat down with him. Once the opening night festivities had concluded, everyone including all of the players stood for the playing of the National Anthem. A few moments later the umpire behind home plate blurted out in a deep voice "Play Ball"! What was once the dream of Shaun O'Leary was now a successful reality. O'Leary was not in attendance for opening night. He would finish his opening weekend barnstorm in New York for a Sunday afternoon double header. During the seventh inning stretch "Take me out to the ballgame" was played. On the scoreboard there was a special announcement. "I'm Tom Wilder with CNN news with a special announcement. The Supreme Court of the United States has just reinstated college sports in the United States effective immediately. The Supreme Court heard arguments from University Presidents, students, athletes and parents concerning the hardships the suspension of college sports has had on their lives and on the financial outlook of the colleges. Preparations for the return of college athletics will begin immediately. Colleges shall have the right to determine which sports they can afford to keep and are free to eliminate the others. College sports will return in the fall of 2031". The entire stadium erupted with cheering along with the rest of the country. Joe Mills shook his head in disbelief. Shaun O'Leary had not only resurrected professional baseball but had also spearheaded the successful drive to return college sports to America. He couldn't wait to talk to O'Leary. The two friends continued watching the game from the dugout and spent the entire nine innings in the team's dugout cheering their team on to an exciting ten to nine victory over the already rival Big Apples. On the way home after the game, Manna asked Floyd if he knew who won and he answered, "Sure I do, New York won". They all laughed. Really in retrospect, everybody won that night.

# Chapter XXII

On the last day of October 2030 Joe Mills left his home to return to his New York newspaper office for the last time. Mr. Wiseman had allowed Joe to leave his office as it was because he was hoping Joe would change his mind and return to his old position. What he didn't know was Joe had unfulfilled promises to his wife Bea. As he looked back on the past year he couldn't believe how much things had changed. It was almost as crazy as 2020, well almost. The loss of his old friend Floyd Rocket Beal in August to Alzheimer's had been devastating. He was happy Beal lived long enough to see the inception of the new league and was able to attend a couple of games before his mind diminished but he wished he'd been able to live into September to see the restart of college football. Of course, if he'd lived long enough to see that, Mills knew he'd wish Beal could see the restart of college basketball. He missed his friend and former co-owner of the New York Empire organization. After Floyd Beal died Mills sold off his portion of the team. Losing his friend had diminished his desire to continue the day to day operations without his friend despite the league's success. Was it ever a success! The debut of the American Baseball League was actually a rousing success. Over eighty percent of the games were sell outs. Every Division Championship game and every American Series game were complete sell outs. As for the competition it couldn't have been any better. In the Division Series the Los Angeles Stars defeated the Houston Energizers four games to three. The Big Apples did the same against the Empires. In the American Series the Big Apples beat the Stars in seven games. Mills knew if Beal was still alive he'd be saying "Those damned old Yankees"! He chuckled at the thought. At seasons end the owners split all of the profits with the league and the players. Owners were happy, players were happy and so were the fans. Fans loved the lower priced tickets and lower cost of concessions. Families were finally able to attend games and could afford to attend more than one game a year. Shaun O'Leary thought these were the major factors in the success of the league but Mills believed playing only on weekends and being able to develop natural rivals due to close proximity were also huge factors. The league was preparing for season number two in April of 2031.

Ron Mills started packing the numerous plastic containers with the contents of his office. He couldn't believe all he'd accumulated over time. He started taking his pictures off the wall. There was a picture of him and Floyd Beal the first time they'd met. They both looked so young and so excited he thought. Right next to it was the last picture he and Beal made together on opening night five months earlier. They both looked so old he thought but still excited. The excitement was still there. The more he looked at the pictures the more he realized how lucky he was. He had photos with more than fifty hall of famers both coaches and players. He sat back down and continued looking at the framed pictures. There he was on his first assignment with World Series Most Valuable Player Daryl Porter. Next to that was a picture of Mills standing between North Carolina Coach Dean Smith and the greatest basketball player of all time Michael Jordon following the Tar Heels 1982 national title victory over Georgetown. He remembered the night well. Jordon a freshman hit the game winning shot giving Coach Smith his first national title. Mills started to realize that the pictures were in a chronological order of some sort. He also realized that if he gazed and took time to remember each picture he'd never get finished in time to be home for Bea's chicken pie. He'd promised her he wouldn't be late. He spent the next three hours packing leaving his perpetual calendar for last. It was the first thing he had took out forty eight years ago and was the last thing he'd pack on his last day. On the drive home he remembered all of the times he'd passed by the same stores, same buildings, and saw many of the same people every day of his life. Did he miss any of this? Not really. He and Bea had plans to settle in their country side home and enjoy their children and grandchildren far away from the city. He knew he'd probably never pass this way again. Forty minutes later he passed by all of the farmland he'd passed every day to get to his house. He pulled into the driveway and was shocked. There was Bea, Manna, Joe's children, grandchildren and even his editor Mr. Wiseman. Good ole Bea was throwing him a surprise retirement party. So that's why he had to be on time. Joe got out of his car and greeted everyone. Everybody enjoyed the chicken pie reminisced about old times and then everyone left. While Bea cleaned up from the party Joe started unloading his car. She stopped Joe in the hall, gave him a big hug and started to tell him how much she'd been looking forward to this day. " Joe, I can't tell you how happy I am. I have waited nearly forty years for the day we could travel and spend more time with the kids and their families. The best part of all is we can spend more time together in that swing. To tell you the truth I was sad when you bought into the new league but I knew it was something you wanted to do with Floyd. I was very sad at Floyd's passing but was really happy when you decided to sell the team". Where do you want to go first" Joe asked her? "After we spend a month in that swing you built I'd like to go to Ocracoke Island in NC. I hear it's a wonderful place. Then after that" before she could finish her sentence the phone rang. Who could that be this late at night they wondered. Bea figured it was just a friend or colleague calling to congratulate Joe on his retirement. Bea answered the phone, "Hey Bea, its Shaun. I wanted to tell Joe congratulations on his official retirement from The Times. I'm sorry I couldn't be at the party. I had meetings scheduled before you told me about the party. I may as well get straight to the point. Besides calling to congratulate Joe, the other reason I am calling is this. Everyone thought I was insane when I wanted to start the ABL and look what a success that's been. People said that college sports would never return but after four years of filing lawsuits college athletics have returned to our college campuses. Now Bea I have an idea on how to bring professional basketball back to America along the same format as the baseball league. I know this is short notice but I have been working on this for quite some time. I need a commissioner for the new league. Someone with a sports background. Someone with experience in starting up a new league. Someone that has the time to do it. Someone like Joe. You know what I'm getting at. Since Joe retired from the newspaper and sold the Empires he'd be the perfect one to lead the new league. After all what else does he have on his agenda? What do you say?" Bea smiled and told Shaun, "no thanks, we are leaving tomorrow on a five year vacation" even if the vacation was in their back-yard she thought to herself. Thirty seconds later she hung up the phone and smiled at Joe. "It was a wrong number" Bea told him. Now where were we she asked. Well, off to our swing first and then its Ocracoke Island, and then where'd you say we were going next?" Joe asked.

# THE END

CPSIA information can be obtained
at www.ICGtesting.com
Printed in the USA
LVHW041035290622
722206LV00005B/78

9 781662 850080